The WRIGHT ONE

ALSO BY K.A. LINDE

WRIGHTS

The Wright Brother
The Wright Boss
The Wright Mistake
The Wright Secret

WRIGHT LOVE DUET

The Wright Love
The Wright One

AVOIDING SERIES

Avoiding Commitment
Avoiding Responsibility
Avoiding Intimacy
Avoiding Decisions
Avoiding Temptation

RECORD SERIES

Off the Record
On the Record
For the Record
Struck from the Record

ALL THAT GLITTERS SERIES

Diamonds
Gold
Emeralds
Platinum
Silver

TAKE ME SERIES

Take Me for Granted
Take Me with You

STAND-ALONE

Following Me

BLOOD TYPE SERIES

Blood Type

ASCENSION SERIES

The Affiliate
The Bound
The Consort

The Wright One

K.A. LINDE

Copyright © 2018 by K.A. Linde
All rights reserved.

Visit my website at www.kalinde.com
Cover Designer: Sarah Hansen, Okay Creations., www.okaycreations.com
Photography: Lauren Perry, Perrywinkle Photography, www.perrywinklephotography.com
Editor and Interior Designer: Jovana Shirley, Unforeseen Editing, www.unforeseenediting.com

No part of this book may be reproduced or transmitted in any form or by any means, electronic or mechanical, including photocopying, recording, or by any information storage and retrieval system without the written permission of the author, except for the use of brief quotations in a book review.

This book is a work of fiction. Names, characters, places, and incidents either are products of the author's imagination or are used fictitiously. Any resemblance to actual persons, living or dead, events, or locales is entirely coincidental.

ISBN-13: 978-1948427234

*To all the fans of the Wright books.
For going on this wonderful journey with me and
allowing me to keep doing my dream job every day!*

One

Sutton

The cemetery was empty this morning.

Save for the ghosts.

And me.

I picked my way through the dusty stones, avoiding the path and staring aimlessly at the rows of the dead. Despite the mid-August Texas weather, it was actually kind of cool with that breeze blowing in. It ruffled the end of my floral skirt and kicked dust into my white tank.

My feet knew the destination well.

My late husband's grave stood like a beacon in the gloom. I stopped before him and replaced the dead flowers I'd brought last time with new ones.

"Hey." I ran my hand along the top of the stone and read Maverick's name etched into the rock. "I've missed you. And I've had a shit week."

I turned my head up to the sky and held back the torrent of emotions that lashed through me. Sadness, depression, despair, anger, fear, rage.

"I started seeing someone," I confessed. "You never knew him. He's the CFO at Wright Construction. He works with Morgan now. I thought it was… right. But it's not."

That was an understatement.

To say the least.

"David Calloway…or David Van Pelt, I guess. He waited a year after you left before approaching me. It felt too real to ignore. We talked. We laughed. We…well, we don't have to talk about that. I confided everything in him. He was so understanding. Mav, I don't get it." I blinked away the tears I'd sworn I would not shed. "He lied to me. He's a liar. He's not a Calloway. He's a Van Pelt."

Maverick had already known the bullshit with the Van Pelts, a family who ran a New York–based investment firm. They'd stolen millions from the Wrights when my dad was running the company, and then they'd been turned over for investment fraud eight years ago. The patriarch of the family and David's father, Broderick Van Pelt was serving a ridiculously long sentence for his crimes.

We hated them. David knew we hated them.

"And he never once told me. He lied about everything in his past. Now, I'm left wondering… who is he?"

I rocked forward and back, trying to calm myself down. Anger was the chief emotion now. I just wanted to unleash it. But I didn't.

"I'm sorry I'm telling you all this. You were my best friend, and now, you're gone. I can't talk to anyone else about this. I'm so mad at him, Mav." I paced in front of the grave. "I want to go back to the house, close the doors, and live in a bubble. It's easier than living in this world."

I threw my arms wide in frustration.

"I put myself out there, and for what? To just get betrayed?" I spat.

I circled back around and saw his name written on the stone. *Maverick Wright*. He'd changed it for me. Even though I'd said I'd change my name, he had known what that name meant. It had been his suggestion. He hadn't been whipped. He'd just loved me.

The wind blew out of my sails. I dropped down, cross-legged, in front of his grave.

"It was so easy for us," I whispered.

My eyes traveled to the tattoo on my wrist. The dandelions blowing in the breeze. I'd gotten it done soon after Maverick's death. My brother Austin and his girlfriend, Julia, had taken me. Maverick had given me a dandelion the first time we were together. He'd said that I was too good for him. And I'd fallen for him on the spot. Insisted on proving him wrong. Things had escalated quickly. Jason had come about unexpectedly. But I'd thought it was fate. I'd thought our little happy family was destiny.

How wrong I was.

About this.

About that.

About David.

"I want it to be easy, Mav. I want dandelions blowing in the breeze. I want sorority events and keg parties and those good times. Now, my sorority friends won't even speak with me. I hardly drink.

You're gone. There are no more good times without you."

I shook my head. Maybe nothing would be as easy as it had been with Maverick. Maybe an easy life wasn't in the cards for me.

"I thought David would be a new beginning."

I dropped my head into my hands and fended off the tears. I wasn't sad. I was pissed. I was devastated. I'd put my heart on the line. If this was living, I didn't want to be a part of it.

All I wanted was to have that carefree lifestyle I'd lived for so long. But I knew it wasn't coming back. That was inevitable now.

"Jason misses you, too," I told Maverick. "He doesn't fully understand yet, but in a way, he does. I wish we were still a family. Everything would be easier if you were here."

But he wasn't here.

It was painful to remind myself of that.

That I was talking to a ghost and hoping for the best.

I'd learned my lesson. Maverick would listen. But I was the only one who could fix my problems.

Two

David

The truth had come out, and I'd lost everything.
Again.

I didn't know why I'd thought this time would be different. That finding out who my parents were wouldn't ruin my life. That their sins wouldn't fall on me...and my sister, Katherine. But they did. They always would.

Of course, I should have told Sutton.

The first time I'd heard how much the Wrights hated the Van Pelts, I should have taken Sutton aside and told her the truth. *I'm a Van Pelt. Those are my parents. They're assholes. I don't claim them. Please, forgive me.*

But I hadn't. Every time I'd tried to talk to her, I'd kept pushing it off. Finding any excuse not to utter the words that I'd been avoiding for eight long years. The family I'd chosen to forget. Then, I'd gotten too far in with Sutton, and I couldn't find my way back out.

The whole thing had been shit luck, too. Jensen knowing Penn Kensington. Penn showing up *here*, in Lubbock, fucking Texas. I'd come here because it was the middle of fucking nowhere. Just went to show that, no matter how far you ran, your past would always catch up with you.

Staring down all the Wrights after Austin punched me in the face and Sutton told me to leave had been miserable. There was no mercy in those faces. They'd support one of their own to the end. And, in that moment, I wasn't the CFO of their family corporation or Morgan's closest friend or Sutton's boyfriend.

I was the enemy.

So, I'd done the only thing I could do. I'd turned around and walked out. Picking up the remains of my shattered dignity and stumbling over what was left of my pride, I'd exited Wright Construction, assuming I'd have to find another place of employment by Monday morning.

Penn had followed me out of the party and apologized over and over. I'd clapped him on the back and assured him it wasn't his fault. He'd done the right thing after that—shut up and gotten me drunk.

Now, I was sitting in my Ferrari outside of Sutton's house with a headache that pounded on my skull. My sunglasses barely kept the morning light from stabbing my retinas and intensifying last night's bad decision.

I'd walked out, defeated, and woken up, determined.

I could walk away again. I could run with my tail between my legs as fast and as far away as I could get from Lubbock and the Wrights. I'd done it before. Twice. Christ, three times if you counted Yale. Running had become second nature. Part of who I was.

Or…I could stay. I could fight. I could win her back.

I had every intention of winning her back.

That was why I was sitting in my car in front of her house like a dumbass.

I ran a shaky hand back through my sandy-blond hair, steeled my nerves, and exited the car. This was going against everything in my nature. The only thing I worked for was my career. And I never had to stay anywhere long for that. I could jump around and be as successful as I was in this moment, but there would never be another Sutton.

Moving up the pathway to her front door felt like a walk of shame. I ignored the ache behind my temples and knocked on the door. I could hear the television on in the living room. The sound of feet rushing across the hardwood floor. Then, I saw a little face peer out through the glass on the side of the door.

"David!" Jason cried upon seeing me.

I smiled and waved at him. Though I knew his presence would only make this harder. Sutton was not going to be happy that I was here. She definitely wasn't going to be happy that her son was happy to see me.

"What did I tell you about going to the door?" I heard Sutton ask sharply.

"Sorry," he murmured, backing away.

"Go watch TV and play with your toys. Mommy will be there in a minute."

A second later, the lock clicked on the door, and she pulled it open a few inches but not all the way. "What do you want?"

For a moment, my breath caught at the sight of her dressed in a floral skirt and white tank. Her brown-blonde ombré hair was tied up in a short ponytail. She was the most beautiful sight I'd ever seen. Willowy, proud, confident. Though she looked at me with wary eyes and had already closed herself off from me, I couldn't deny her beauty, her tenacity, her strength. All the things that had made me fall for her.

"David?" she asked cautiously.

"I came to apologize."

She rolled her eyes skyward. "I don't need your apology. I need you to leave."

She started to close the door in my face, and I moved on instinct. I slapped my hand on the door, keeping it from closing. Her eyes rounded. Her mouth popped open in surprise. Had she thought I wouldn't fight for her? I was going to prove her wrong.

"Let go."

"No, I want to talk. Five minutes."

"I don't have five minutes." Her eyes strayed to her son playing like a maniac in the living room, running around in circles and making airplane noises.

"I know. I understand."

"You clearly don't," she said on a scoff.

"I'm sorry. I'm really sorry, Sutton. I tried to tell you. I know that doesn't make up for the fact that I didn't tell you, but no moment was ever right. And I did tell you that what was going on with my parents was complicated."

"Complicated means you had a fight and haven't reconciled," she hissed. "Not that your family is infamous for stealing money, and your father is in prison for investment fraud."

"Are those two things really that different?"

"I can't talk about this with you."

"Please, I'm sorry. I care about you, Sutton. I want to make this right."

"If you wanted to make this right, then you wouldn't have *lied* to me about everything."

"Look, I don't agree with my parents. I don't agree with anything they did. I already told you that I don't side with them. That's why Katherine and I have been estranged this long. I left them. I left."

"God, you honestly think that I'm upset just because you're a Van Pelt? That it's about who your family is? News flash: we don't choose our family. My mom died when I was one, and my dad was a raging alcoholic, absentee father. I know all about fucked up families, if you're unaware. I care that you *lied* to me about it. That you had me fall for one person when that isn't even who you are."

"This *is* who I am," I told her.

But I could see that it didn't register. It couldn't register. She had already internally shut that door. Walked away from any hope I had of righting these wrongs. She'd been hurt before. This was just one too many.

"You're a Van Pelt, David, which is honestly just icing on the cake of this entire thing."

"I might have grown up as a Van Pelt, but I changed my name for a reason. That's not who I am anymore."

"You actively avoided telling me."

"Because I don't tell anyone!" I cried, losing some of my chill. My headache was a savage beast threatening my resolve on this subject.

She took a step back from me. "Don't yell at me."

I blew out a breath and ran my hand back through my hair. "I'm sorry. I'm not yelling. I just feel so dumb. Like I had this whole speech planned, and none of it's coming out right."

She crossed her arms and shrugged. She glanced at Jason again, trying to avoid eye contact with me.

I should have expected this. On some level, I guessed I had. She hadn't wanted to talk to me at the party yesterday. Why would she want to give me a chance today? Her anger was warranted. I hadn't lied to her, but at the same time…I'd lied to her. I'd known that keeping this secret was a bad idea. That it would hurt us, but I hadn't been able to let go. I'd carried it around with me for so long that opening up that wound again felt insurmountable. Why ruin the one good thing in my life? Well, my silence had done that just as certainly.

"The only reason I never told you is because I was worried about how you would react," I finally said on a sigh.

"This is how you knew I'd react," she told me. "And you didn't want to face that."

"Would you believe me if I said that I never wanted this to happen?"

"Yes, but that doesn't change anything. I've been hurt enough for one lifetime, David. Can you save me from the rest of it?" Her eyes finally met mine. Hurt. I'd hurt her. "Nothing you say is going to change my mind. Now, remove your hand from my door."

I pulled my hand from the door and straightened where I was standing. "Sutton—"

"Please stop," she said, chewing on her bottom lip.

I could see her resolve weakening a fraction. I wanted to press and demand more from her. But that pain on her face said I needed to give her more time.

"All right." I stepped back. "I'm not going to stop fighting for you."

"I don't want you to fight for me." She slowly eased the door closed until the lock clicked back in place.

She might have said it, but I didn't believe her. She needed to come to terms with what had happened. She needed the full explanation of why I was estranged from my fucked up family. We could recover from this. I could change her mind. But, first, I needed to make sure that I still had a job.

Three

David

Without calling her, I knew Morgan would be at the office.

My boss was the biggest workaholic I'd ever met, and that was really saying something in business. She used to be even worse before she started dating Patrick, but he was an understanding dude. That meant she was at the office nearly every weekend. After missing a couple of days for Emery's bachelorette party, it was almost a given that she'd be back in to catch up.

What I hadn't expected was to find Jensen and Penn in the conference room along with her. Just great. This was going to be fun.

"All the people I wanted to see in one place," I said. All heads popped up to stare at me.

"David," Morgan said with pursed lips, "why don't you come in?"

I strode forward into the conference room I'd docked hundreds of hours in during the last year. I'd thought Lubbock would be different. But the past never really stayed in the past.

"We were just talking about you," she continued.

"I'm sure that was a lively discussion," I deadpanned.

"Penn was filling us in on how much of a good guy you are," Jensen added.

"Thanks." I nodded at Penn.

But I didn't need him to go to bat for me. I appreciated it, but it wasn't necessary. Penn was a stand-up guy. He'd gotten out of New York City high society, too. Well…as best he could while still being a Kensington with a mother who was the mayor and his brother, Court, the royal fuckup of the Upper East Side. I'd fallen into Court's orbit after my best friend, Holli, killed herself in high school. Penn was vouching for me off of my sister, Katherine's, good graces since they were best friends, but I didn't actually know how highly he thought of me after spending so much time with Court.

"I know that I outed you, and I wanted to do what I could to smooth the situation over," Penn said.

He slid his hands into the pockets of his suit that I knew cost more than the down payment of many houses. There was money, and then there was Kensington money.

"He wouldn't have needed to smooth anything over if you'd talked to us," Morgan snapped.

"Morgan," Jensen said.

"I know; I know. We said we'd be calm and sensible about this. When have I ever been calm and sensible?"

"Never," I assured her.

"Hey now!"

I couldn't help it; I grinned.

Jensen sighed dramatically. "I don't know why you didn't tell us."

"Well, at first, I didn't know you cared that much about the Van Pelt name. I'd left already and sealed my name change, so I could start fresh on my own. Then, when I found out how you felt, it was too late. I realized how much you hated my family, and I was stuck."

"We understand hating family. We understand family obligation. We understand keeping secrets even," Jensen clarified. "But it comes down to lying on your application and then...hurting our sister."

"Sutton is devastated," Morgan chimed in.

"I know. I just saw her."

"You went to see her? Are you insane?" Morgan asked.

"When it comes to her? Yes."

Morgan rolled her eyes. "Oh, boy."

"And I didn't lie on my application," I added. "My legal name is David Calloway. I am no longer David Van Pelt anywhere. Background checks don't pull it up, and unless I told someone, no one would ever know. That is how I wanted it to be."

"So, you were going to just live this...lie?" Morgan asked on a sigh.

"This isn't a lie."

"It is," she said. "If you can't see it, then how are you ever going to get her back?"

I shut my mouth at that. Those words weren't the ones I'd been expecting from her. I'd thought she'd be pissed and never want to speak to me again, like Sutton. But, now, it sounded like she wanted me to fight back.

"This conversation isn't about Sutton," Jensen reminded Morgan.

"Except that it is."

"Company first."

Morgan inhaled deeply and then started again, "We're not firing you, if that's why you look worried."

"I was."

"And you'd better not fucking quit," she said, pointing her finger at me.

"I hadn't planned to."

"Good. Because I am not training another person to do my job again. It was messy enough when I moved you into CFO," she said dramatically.

"Plus, we have no grounds," Jensen added. He shook his head at Morgan. They must have had this conversation, and Morgan kept veering off course. "She's the CEO, of course, but I'm on the board. I don't want a legal battle."

"Another legal battle," Morgan muttered.

"This reminds me why I don't go home," Penn said, dragging out a chair and sinking into a seat.

"Aren't families the greatest?" I asked sarcastically.

Morgan and Jensen grinned at each other. They argued all the time, but they loved each other. That was a fact. The Wrights were closer than any family I'd ever known.

"Anyway, I'm not leaving the company. And I'm glad you don't want to kick me out of the job. Or...I guess, more specifically, you don't want to spend time training someone else. That's convenient for me."

"Yeah, but Austin is still pissed about Sutton," Morgan told me.

"And Sutton is pissed," I added.

"Yeah. And you probably made it worse."

"Probably. I was kind of an idiot."

"What else is new?" Morgan asked. "I mean, I get why she's pissed. I thought we were friends, and you couldn't even tell me."

"I didn't tell anyone. Ever."

"I mean...I get that, but it doesn't make it any better. I still feel like you don't trust me with who you really are or you don't want me to really get to know you. And I don't even really like you," she said with a short laugh.

"Liar," I said.

She waved her hand in a characteristic Morgan fashion that said, *Whatever*. "All I'm saying is that, if I'm frustrated with you, imagine how Sutton feels."

"Not good," Jensen clarified. "Women generally don't like to be lied to. As a rule."

"Even I know that," Penn said with a smile.

"Plus, after what she went through..." Morgan let the implication hang between us.

Just over a year ago, Sutton had lost her husband. I was painfully aware that I was the first person she'd let in since that happened. That she had opened up and wanted to be with me. And then I'd broken that trust. Put her back on the defensive. Ruined any progress I'd made on helping her find love again.

"I know," I finally said.

And I really did.

She had every reason to feel like she couldn't trust me. But I'd grovel if I had to. I'd show her that I wasn't the monster she'd made me out to be.

"You're a shithead. You know that, right?" Morgan asked.

"Yeah. Pretty much."

"But we're not firing you."

"That's good. I couldn't find a better boss."

Morgan rolled her eyes. "Suck-up."

"Flattery never hurt anyone."

"Jesus Christ," Jensen said. "You two together are like an old married couple. When I hired David, I assumed this was a stepping-stone job for him. With his credentials, it made sense. But looks like you're here to stay."

"That's the plan," I told him.

Jensen stuck his hand out, and we shook. "Good to hear it. Now, I need to get home to my rather frazzled fiancée. This wedding cannot come soon enough."

"You're the one who invited the whole town," Morgan accused.

"It could be family only, and we all know Emery would be this way."

Morgan laughed. "True."

"I'm going to head out, too. I'm meeting a few colleagues for dinner." Penn shook my hand, too. "If you want to meet up again before I leave, let me know."

"Sure thing."

We watched them both walk out of the room and then turned back to face the other.

"So…what kind of chance do I have at this thing with Sutton?"

"Give her some space," Morgan told me. "Like…a lot of space. Maybe she'll come around."

"I don't like dealing in uncertainties."

"Tough shit."

I laughed. "Fine, fine. Space it is. But not too much space."

"No," Morgan agreed, "not too much."

And then we shared a secret smile. She might be pissed at me, but in that moment, we were in on this together.

Four

Sutton

Monday morning blues were a real thing.
Who had decided that the week started on Monday anyway?

At least waking bright and early gave me an excuse to get out of the house and away from my thoughts. It was hard to think about anything, except measurements and mixing, when I was at the bakery, Death by Chocolate. And my boss, Kimber, at least didn't have any designs on talking about what had happened with David at the party this weekend. Another blessing.

It was almost three when I finally came up from my working stupor long enough to check my phone and find out I had two missed calls from Morgan.

I told Kimber I was taking a break and headed out back. Morgan answered on the second ring.

"Finally," she said.

"Hey, Mor. What's up?"

"I need you to come by the office this afternoon."

"Why?"

A panic rose in my chest. The office meant David. It meant facing him again. I'd barely had enough strength to tell him to leave the last time. If he'd kept talking, I had been sure I'd crumble. Just seeing his beautiful face had made me weak when I wanted to be so strong. I was so angry with him about everything, and yet I wanted him to comfort me. It was this strange and irritating duality.

"Family stuff."

"Do I really have to?" I asked. "I'm kind of trying to avoid David."

"He's going to be out of the office."

"Oh. You didn't fire him, did you?"

"Do you want us to?"

"No," I said honestly. "I think what he did was wrong, but would you even have grounds?"

"God, you sound just like Jensen."

"Isn't that normally your job?"

"Normally," she conceded. "And, no, we're not firing him. He's walking on eggshells in the office, is all."

"Except he's not in the office this afternoon?"

"Nope. See you around five?"

"All right, but I can't stay long. Jenny has Jason, and then I'm going to look at daycares."

"Oh," Morgan said, dragging out the syllable. "Ditching the nanny?"

"It's not ideal, but Jenny wants to be a pharmacist, and I don't trust many people with Jason. By many people, read *no one*. Let alone at my house all day. So, if I can't fill her shoes, I'd rather have him in a professional setting with other children."

The WRIGHT ONE

"That'd be good for him."

"Probably." Though the thought made me nauseated. Giving up control was next to impossible. "Well, I'll see you soon."

"See you then!"

I was late.

Not on purpose, but finishing up at the bakery had taken longer than anticipated with all the college kids coming back into town. I was only a couple of years removed from that life, and already, the divide felt like a giant chasm.

Stashing my apron in the backseat of my blue Audi TT, I exited the car and stared up at the building that had wrecked my new, wonderful life. It was on the top-floor restaurant of Wright Construction where I'd found out that David had lied to me. Truthfully, I wasn't looking forward to entering those doors again. Or dealing with whatever new mess Morgan had discovered for our family. Because, Lord knew, there was always something.

But I held my head up and strode inside anyway.

The afternoon crowd had already cleared their desks. The elevator was empty as I took it up to the second to top floor to see my sister. I really hoped this only lasted a minute. I was burned out on family time.

I tiptoed to David's office and peeked inside. I let out a breath. Okay, he really was out of the office. Everything was dark inside. No David.

I hurried past Morgan's office and went straight to the conference room since that was where all family meetings were held. It was probably going to be about David even though they weren't firing him. Just what I didn't want to discuss.

With a sigh, I knocked on the door and then entered. To my surprise, Morgan was sitting on the conference table, dangling her black high heels. She smiled at me when I entered, which was the moment I realized this was a fucking setup.

My eyes strayed around the room and found David standing in the corner, staring down at his computer. At my entrance, his head popped up. His eyes rounded in shock, and then he turned on Morgan in accusation.

"What did you do?" I asked.

"How could you?" David asked at nearly the same time.

"Sutton, why don't you come inside and shut the door?"

I gritted my teeth and took a step into the room. But I left the door gaping. I wanted a quick escape, just in case.

"You set me up," I accused.

"Both of us up," David amended. "I had nothing to do with this."

"I know. I did this all on my own. I was sure that it would take weeks before either of you stubborn asses budged enough to have this conversation," Morgan said.

"You don't get to just interfere in our lives," I said. "We're not puppets. This is real life, Mor."

"I know it is. If someone had forced Patrick and me into a room, I would have been with him earlier. We would have been happy. And I'm a cynic, but I'm hoping that happens for you two. You're my sister and closest friend. If it doesn't work out, it doesn't work out, but I'm not going to say I didn't try to help."

"When did you become a hopeless romantic?" I asked.

"I blame all of this on Patrick," she said with a small smile. "Now...talk. Figure it out."

Morgan tilted her head at David and then brushed my shoulder on her way out the door. She let it click shut behind her.

I leaned back against the door and let my purse drop to the floor. My eyes stayed on it as I waited to figure out what the hell was going to happen. I mean, I didn't want to have this conversation. I'd been duped. My sister was a traitor.

"I'm sorry about this," David finally said, breaking the silence. "I didn't tell her to do this, and would never intentionally push you into this kind of situation. In fact, she was the one who said that I should give you space."

"Must have changed her mind."

"She means well?"

I snorted and glanced up at him. "Yeah, she does."

"I mean, I didn't set this up, but since we're here…"

"Yeah." I shrugged. "If I had it my way, I'd just go. I have to pick up Jason soon."

"You can go if you want."

It sounded like that was the last thing he'd wanted to say. Yet he'd said it anyway.

"I hate that I can't trust you," I finally said.

"I hate that you feel that way."

My eyes dragged up to his, which were honey hazel and full of remorse. His sandy-blond hair was flipped to one side, and a frown marred his perfect face. His strong jawline was clenched, as if he couldn't decide on a course of action. He seemed frozen in place, unable to move forward. And I felt like I was in that same place.

And none of it helped that he was so damn attractive. Well over six feet tall with a dazzling smile. A body that showed he worked out religiously. He would definitely survive a zombie apocalypse with the amount of time he spent running every day. I knew for a fact that he had six-pack abs and muscles in all the right places to make me swoon. That V that led south was my undoing. Yet I couldn't go there right now.

I couldn't think about his body or the incredible way he used it or the way our lips melded together, as if they had been made for each other. None of those things changed the fact that I felt betrayed. I'd opened my heart, and he'd stomped on it.

So, we stood there in silence. Tension building between us. Frustration pooling in my stomach. My hands shook at my sides. I was cursing myself for the second cupcake I'd had that afternoon. A sugar buzz was just what I needed right now.

"I guess…I don't have anything to say," I muttered. I grabbed my bag off the ground and turned toward the door. "This was a mistake."

"Wait!" David rushed across the room. He put his hand out to prevent me from opening the door.

"Is this turning into a thing for you?"

"If you want to go, go," he said, hovering over me. "But I don't want you to."

The WRIGHT ONE

It was that moment I realized how close our bodies were to one another. I was half-turned toward the door. My hand still on the knob. His body was practically covering my petite frame. The heat from our bodies mingled in the small distance. His hand that wasn't holding the door moved to my elbow. It was gentle, almost hesitant, but still, it sent electricity up my arm.

Suddenly, it was as if all the air had been sucked out of the room. I dropped my hand from the door and faced him. He must have felt the energy crashing between us. A current that was as intense as it was unshakable.

For a second, I thought he would pull back. Let me pass. Allow me to escape this static that was sure to set aflame. Instead, he pressed forward toward me. Bridged that short distance until my heart rate ratcheted ever upward, my pulse beating a tattoo against my throat. My mouth went dry. My insides squeezed.

Then, there was just a dull ringing in my ears. Anything could have been happening around me, but all I knew was David. It was terrifying and exhilarating, and...it desperately needed to stop.

But I could no more sever this connection than the moon could stop orbiting Earth.

Conjuring a cataclysmic event to disrupt my orbit with David was tantamount to impossible. It just was. And we just were.

Even when I didn't want us to be.

"Sutton," he breathed softly.

His head hung down in the small space between us, so we were nearly at eye-level. My own head tilted up to meet his passionate gaze.

His hand moved up from my elbow and over my shoulder before caressing my cheek. I should stop this. I should...do something.

"We should stop," I told him.

"Just let me explain. Please, I don't open up like this, Sutton. I've never talked to anyone about any of this before. Not even my own sister."

"About being a Van Pelt? I'm pretty sure your sister already knew that."

"No, about why I'm living this double life. Why I can't open up to anyone. I mean, I knew telling you would upset you, and sure, part of it was that I didn't want to piss you off. But the other side is that I don't know how to be open about that kind of thing."

"I think you open your mouth and say, *Sutton, I'm a Van Pelt.*"

He sighed, leaning his head forward until it brushed against my forehead. A tingle shot through my body.

"I wish it were that easy."

"You can make it that easy."

He nodded, meeting my gaze again. "Then, let me try."

"I..."

"Please, Sutton. Let me try to be the man you deserve."

I knew walking away was the smart idea. That he didn't deserve the chance to explain anything to me right now. That I wanted to scream with anger that we'd only gotten to this moment because he was outed. That he'd gotten caught.

But, instead, I just stood there as his lips moved closer to mine. As my world ground to a stop. Until nothing else mattered but that slow-motion movement.

The touch of those lips.

That undeniable temptation.

"No," I breathed.

"Sutton, please," he said. "This is right between us. You know it is. You can feel it. You can feel it here." He pressed his hand to my heart and felt the powerful rhythm.

Our lips almost touched again. A hairbreadth apart. I wanted to give in. It'd be so easy. But it wouldn't erase everything that had gone on between us.

"I need more time," I told him.

Then, I did the only thing I could to save myself. I pulled open the door and fled.

Five

Sutton

I rushed down the hallway and straight into an open elevator. I could sense David behind me. He could easily catch me. Stick his hand in the elevator to keep it from going downstairs. Anything.

Instead, he stood in front of the elevator door and let his hand drop. Our eyes stayed locked.

For a second, I almost thought about stopping the inevitable. I could stay and hear him out. I could let him explain away why he'd lied to me the entire time we were dating. I wasn't ready to talk. Morgan had known that. David had known that. So, I did nothing. And he disappeared from view as the doors slowly eased closed.

I slammed my hand on the elevator wall and screamed into the closed metal tube. How the fuck did my world keep shattering like this? Why couldn't any of it be goddamn easy?

Tears threatened to spill from my eyes. I choked them back, swiping at the traitorous ducts. The last thing I wanted to do was cry. Again. I was so beyond *done* with crying. All I needed was to get home to my son, eat an entire container of ice cream, and get over myself.

I was tired of feeling like a victim. I was standing in the story of my life. When would I start to feel like the strong heroine? And not just the shell of the woman I had been?

The elevator deposited me on the bottom floor of Wright, and I rushed out to my car. Once I slid into the driver's seat, I texted Morgan.

Don't ever do that to me again.

I was just trying to help.

Don't try to help. I don't need your help.

Sut, I'm sorry. If you want to talk, I'm here.

I turned off the phone without answering and tossed it into my purse. Talk? Yeah, no. I didn't want to talk. And I wasn't going to deal with any more of her bullshit. Morgan was the CEO of Wright Construction. She knew exactly who she was and what she wanted and how to get it. How could someone like that possibly understand how I was feeling or what I wanted? She might be my sister. She might have helped raise me. But I was fucking tired of my siblings in my business. So tired of being the sad widow everyone pitied. I just wanted to forget any of this shit with David had ever happened.

The WRIGHT ONE

I sped home. My mind on the encounter with David. He couldn't open up. But why? There had to be a reason he was like that. Was it from living in New York City? I'd seen *Gossip Girl*; I knew the dramatized version of what it was like to live on the Upper East Side. Did it have something to do with losing his best friend, Holli, to suicide in high school? Or was it just because he was a Van Pelt? And Van Pelts were liars.

Whoop-whoop.

"Oh fuck!" I groaned as red and blue lights flashed in my rearview mirror.

I used every four-letter word I had in my vocabulary as I veered toward the side of the road. I pulled out my license and registration and waited with my window rolled down.

"Ma'am, do you know how fast you were going?" the officer asked.

I glanced up, ready to put on the waterworks and suddenly laughed instead. "Gregory McKinnon?"

His face split into a smile. "Hey, Sutton."

It was one of Annie's many exes. But I'd actually liked this one. "It's good to see you. I don't know how fast I was going. I just went through a bad breakup, and my mind is not here."

He frowned. "I'm sorry to hear that. Especially after…" He let the silence drag out for a second. "Well…you know…your husband."

I nearly choked on that word. Yeah, my husband. And a breakup. Man, I was a winner.

"Look, I'd just give you a warning, but you were booking it." He gave me a sad smile.

"Sure. Of course."

Gregory took my license and registration and came back a few minutes later with a shiny new ticket. He put me at nine under. I was sure I'd been going faster than that. Sympathy points.

I said good-bye to him and then went the exact speed limit all the way home. I parked the Audi in the garage and barreled into the house, waving the speeding ticket in my hand.

"Can you believe this?" I cried.

Jenny stood in the living room with Jason, doing some silly dance. "What's that?"

That was when I noticed Annie was plopped down on my couch. She was filing her nails and glanced up expectantly.

"A freaking speeding ticket." I pointed it at Annie. "From your ex."

"Which one?" she asked.

"Gregory McKinnon."

"Oh, he's still hot. I didn't know he was a cop." She contemplatively tapped her finger on her lips. "I need to up my stalking skills."

"Stop that! He's a jerk who gave me a ticket after what I went through…"

Jen's and Annie's eyebrows rose at the last part.

"After you went through what?" Jen asked.

My hand dropped dramatically. The ticket was a thorn in my side. I wanted to tear it up and watch it fall to ashes. But, obviously, I couldn't.

"Nothing," I murmured. I turned to Jason, who had toddled over to me. "Come here!"

I wrapped my arms around my growing boy and lifted him onto my hip. He wrapped his arms around my neck and squeezed me until I felt like I couldn't breathe. And I didn't care one bit. Who needed to breathe when my baby wanted hugs? He'd grow up soon enough and not want them as much. I'd take all I could get right now.

"You know we don't buy what you're selling," Annie said.

"Like, not at all," Jenny said.

"I don't want to talk about it."

"From that outburst, I'm guessing you need to talk about it," Jenny added.

"Yep. What she said," Annie said.

I groaned and sat Jason back down, crumpling onto the floor next to him. His mind was always going, going, going, and I played the new game he'd invented with the blocks. Really, I was evading the questions and pointed stares. Working up the courage to talk about it.

"Morgan set up me and David so that we were alone at Wright this afternoon."

"Oh, boy," Jenny said.

"Yeah. He came over Saturday to try to convince me that we should be together or whatever, but I told him I needed time and slammed the door in his face. Then, Morgan did this, and...we almost kissed."

"Ooh la la," Annie said. "So, are you getting back together?"

"No." I shook my head. "I freaked out and left."

Jenny sighed. "Did he say anything other than trying to kiss you?"

"Yeah. I mean, he said he has a hard time opening up. Some shit happened in his past. Plus, his parents are the freaking Van Pelts. They're notorious liars. I doubt they were great parents. But I just think that's an excuse."

"Maybe a reason," Jenny said.

"Fine, a reason. Whatever. But it doesn't justify what he did."

"No, it doesn't," Annie agreed. "Let's be clear. This guy infiltrated your life and made you fall for him, and the entire time, he was living a double life. How could you be with someone like that?"

I opened my mouth and closed it. I couldn't. That was what I'd been saying since I found out. He'd lied to me. Whether or not he'd thought it would be hard to be honest with me, I felt betrayed. And I couldn't just *stop* feeling that way.

"Whoa!" Jenny said. "Calm that down. He didn't infiltrate anyone's life. He's not a spy. Don't be dramatic, Annie."

"I'm not being dramatic. He's an asshole!"

"Asshole!" Jason repeated.

"Annie!" Jenny and I said at the same time.

"Sorry. Sorry!"

"We don't say that word," I told Jason. "Not until you're older."

He gave me an incredulous look, as if he were now going to say asshole all the time and I couldn't stop him. *Thanks, Annie!*

"David came here for a job. He probably didn't plan on starting a relationship. Are you sure he even knew that Wright was associated with his parents? Or that you hated them like you do? It's possible that he didn't even know."

"Maybe," I conceded.

"But, once he found out, he should have said something," Annie added.

"Yes, but I don't think he was purposefully malicious."

"White lies are still lies," I muttered.

"That's right!" Annie said. "I freaking hate guys who lie. Like, argh! They make me want to scream. How dare they lie to you like that! As if you don't care one bit whether or not they have a girlfriend or whatever."

I exchanged a confused look with Jenny. "Uh... Annie? What are you talking about?"

Her freckled cheeks turned a soft pink, contrasting with her red hair. "So...I might just be anti-guy right now."

"Aren't you always?" Jen asked with an arched eyebrow.

"Well, you know I slept with your cousin, Jordan, when he was in town."

"We're *all* aware," I said.

"He...has a girlfriend back in Vancouver."

My eyes widened. "Oh!"

"What an asshole!" Jenny said.

"Asshole!" Jason repeated.

"Dear God, y'all!" I cried.

We all broke down into giggles. It was impossible not to. Jason wasn't a particularly loquacious kid, but when he latched on to a word, he really went for it.

"Okay, Jordan is clearly...not a good guy," I said. "That sucks, Annie."

"I just...really liked him. Sorry to break into this whole jerkfest about David with my own problems."

"I appreciate it. It's nice to know I'm not the only one, honestly."

Jenny laughed. "Hardly. I might or might not have been talking to Julian while he was here."

Annie and I squealed in delight.

Both of my best friends into both of my cousins. Go figure!

She held her hand up. "But I don't think he sees me that way. He rightfully is too worried about his mom's cancer, moving to Texas with her, and getting a new job. Plus…cancer. I don't blame him for not wanting someone…like me."

"Shut up!" Annie cried.

"You're awesome, Jen," I added.

"I'm shy and reserved, and I might not even get into pharmacy school. You two have it all together."

"Wow, we are all…just messed up."

Annie nodded. "We really are."

"I think that," Jen said softly, "if David is going to fight for you despite all that happened, then maybe you should let him."

"I do love a good grovel," Annie said with a mischievous smile.

"Good guys are hard to come by," Jenny said.

"Impossible!" Annie added.

"Yeah," I agreed. I'd had one. The perfect good guy, and look at how that had turned out. "Maybe I should talk to him. I think, through all my rage, I didn't really give him a fair shot to explain."

"Uh…I wouldn't have either," Annie said.

I chuckled. "I'm still pissed, but we did have something, didn't we?"

Jenny nodded. "You did."

"I guess I owe him the chance to tell me the truth even if he wouldn't before. If he really opens up, then I'll see where it goes."

"Just make him work for it," Annie said with a wink.

"And be gentle with yourself," Jen said. "It takes a lot of strength to give someone a second chance. I know that might be hard for you."

I nodded. I'd already lost the love of my life once. I'd seen my brothers and sister fail horribly at love time and time again. I'd seen them come back, kicking and screaming for the person they loved. But I hadn't been able to do that. Nothing could have saved Maverick. We never had a second chance. Maybe… just maybe I could see if that was in the cards for me and David.

Six

David

Three days of radio silence from Sutton.

I'd clearly fucked this entire thing up.

I hadn't pushed her since she ran out on me on Monday afternoon. She needed her space. She needed to figure this out for herself. Even if that meant she decided not to be with me. I didn't want that option, and I was going to do what I could to avoid that, but if that was her choice, I would respect her enough to live by it.

Morgan had apologized for setting us up like that. She'd had good intentions, but it had totally botched whatever headway I'd been making. Now, Sutton was *completely* avoiding me…and Morgan, as far as she'd said. She felt really bad about the whole thing. But the fault still remained with me.

I needed to figure out what my next move would be. I couldn't show up with her favorite flowers and hope for the best. I'd fucked that move up with my hangover. Half-cocked plans were out of the question.

Sutton was...special. I'd never cared for anyone like her. I mean, fuck, I wanted to stay in Lubbock, Texas, for her. This desolate, dusty desert was anything but ideal compared to where I'd lived in the past. It was probably as close as I could get to the opposite of New York City and San Francisco. And yet, when I thought about it, all I had was fondness. And she was the reason.

I'd told the truth when I said that opening up was hard for me. It felt a bit like taking a razor blade to a vein and hoping for the best. Once all my secrets were out, would I really be better for it? Or would it be my demise?

Those thoughts swirled through my head all day as I drudged through seemingly meaningless work memos.

My phone pinged next to me, and I realized that I'd completely neglected it again. I tended to internalize all my problems. When shit got tough, I would go into my head and forget that the outside world existed. It was an awesome quality for work, as I could dig in until I figured everything out. Not so great for life outside of Wright Construction.

I had several missed calls and a text from Katherine.

> *Funny story. I ran into Penn. He said he saw you and accidentally screwed up your life there. Everything okay? Coming home yet?*

I gritted my teeth at the implication that New York was still home. I'd spent eight long years trying to put the city behind me and everything I'd been and done there along with it.

My sister, like Morgan, meant well…usually. Okay, maybe it was more like *sometimes*. She'd grown up on the Upper East Side, just like I had. No one left there unmarked by the black taint that permeated Fifth Avenue.

I kept scrolling. I'd respond some other time.

Then, I saw a notification flash on my screen.

Superhero Movie

Friday, 7:00 p.m.

Be there! Prepare for hot Hemsworth abs!

I blinked. Then, blinked again.

Sutton had surreptitiously added a note into my calendar for the second movie we'd planned to see together. With everything going on, it had completely slipped my mind.

Our first movie together had started this entire thing between us. She'd tried to cancel, worrying that it was a date when she wasn't ready to start dating yet. Or at least, she hadn't warmed to the idea. Then, it had ended in a kiss and snowballed from there. I didn't know what she wanted now. I probably should let it go and reach out to her when she was ready. But this seemed like an opportunity.

My fingers stalled on the words I wanted to send to her. *Would it be presumptuous to force myself into her life before she was ready? And what if she already had plans to take someone else? Did I even want to know if she was backing out?*

Part of me wanted to push. But that hadn't done me any good last time. Fuck, the last two times. It only pushed her further away. And I didn't know how to bring her closer any other way. This was territory that I wasn't familiar with. How could I reach someone who didn't want to be reached?

I tossed the phone down onto my desk. I couldn't do it. She needed to come to me. And she wouldn't do that if I rushed back into her life. Plus, I wasn't ready to hear if she was taking someone else. If she really meant everything that she'd said. Because more time I could give, but having her out of my life forever wasn't an option. Not one I could stomach.

With my head buried in my work again, I was halfway through this memo when a new text buzzed from my phone.

I carelessly glanced over at it. Then, my eyes widened in shock.

We still on for the movie tomorrow?

Well, *that* was an unexpected text message. *Sutton still wants to go to the movie with me? After all of this?* I wasn't about to turn that down or second-guess it in the least.

Yep. 7 p.m.?

See you there.

And that was that.
What the actual fuck?
After all that wondering, she just acted like nothing was out of the norm. Well, all I knew was

that this movie was going to be really fucking interesting.

Our movie was at Alamo Drafthouse, as it had been last time. It was the kind of place where you showed up early even though it had assigned seating. The food was good, the atmosphere was fun, and the staff was excellent. I showed up twenty minutes before the show and waited for Sutton to arrive.

Couples and families passed me with giant smiles on their faces. One guy even wished me good luck. A girl made an *aww* sound when she saw the giant bouquet of daises I had in my hand. Apparently, I was a hit. I might as well be in a John Hughes movie, holding a boom box over my head, for all the attention it was getting me.

But it was Sutton's face that made all the mild humiliation worthwhile. She was fighting a grin when she wandered up to me in jean shorts and a yellow tank top with a jean jacket tucked under her arm.

"Hey," she murmured when she saw me.

"Hey. These are for you."

She took them from me and blushed a pretty shade of pink. "You, uh, didn't have to do this."

"No guy ever has to buy a girl flowers. He does it because he wants to."

"Well, this isn't...you know. This is...just a movie."

"Everything with you is more than just a *just*."

She frowned down at the flowers and then nervously glanced around her, as if she didn't want anyone to see her holding them. "Why don't we get our seats?"

"Sure."

Sutton pulled up our seats on her phone and led me into one of the large auditoriums and all the way up to the top row. Her favorite. We were the first people up there with a handful of other couples scattered around the room. A few were even dressed like the Avengers. Pretty in-depth cosplay, too. Impressive.

"Seems I forgot my costume," I said, trying to break the thick layer of awkwardness that had formed between us.

Sutton made a noncommittal sound.

I sighed and figured I might as well break the ice for real. "I guess I should ask…why did you still come to this with me?"

"Well, I had the tickets," she said, not meeting my eyes.

"You could have taken Annie."

She shook her head. "Actually, I couldn't. She's at orientation this weekend for medical school. She's super booked, doing…I don't know…doctor things."

"Oh, I see. I'm second choice again."

"I suppose, last time, you were first choice because I was tired of Annie only being here to look at hot guys."

"And this time?"

She shrugged. "This time…I don't know."

But, when she said it, she was looking at me. And I could see that she was being cautious around me, but she wasn't pulling back. She wasn't retreating. She was still at a comfortable distance. But we were here. Together. That was something.

THE WRIGHT ONE

"I'll take it."

The moment was broken by the cheery employee who came to take our orders. I got us a giant bowl of popcorn, two waters, and a root beer float for Sutton. He nodded his head at us and then disappeared once more.

Sutton turned her body to face me and sighed. "Okay. I'm not being entirely fair to you."

"Do you have a reason to be fair to me?"

"It's just that I feel like, when I first found out about you, I might have overreacted. I mean, I feel justified in my anger, but the things I said and did, that wasn't right."

"I understood where you were coming from with it all."

She turned away from me and pulled on her jacket. I could see that this conversation was hard for her. She probably didn't even want to be having it.

"I feel like I owe you the chance to explain. I don't know that it will change my mind or make me feel differently, but I'll never know if I don't hear you out."

I stared back at her in surprise. For the last week, I had been certain she was never going to let me explain. And my reasons for hiding my identity might not make her feel any better.

But at least she was giving me a second chance.

Giving *us* a second chance.

Seven

Sutton

We walked out of the movie. The daisies were in my hand between us. Almost a barrier. But not quite.

I couldn't believe that I'd actually been able to spit that all out to him. That we'd had that conversation and sat through a two-and-a-half-hour movie without trying to make out with each other's faces. We'd been at Wright, and I'd barely been able to hold it together. But, somehow, back in that movie theater, we'd made it. The physical connection was there, as ever.

It was the emotional one that my heart was balancing on a tightrope. I didn't know whether I'd make a misstep and plummet into the depths below.

"So…" I murmured. "Some movie."

"Honestly? I think I'm going to have to see it again."

"Why is that? Didn't get your fill of the hot men?"

"I was a little distracted," he said, purposefully meeting my eyes.

I couldn't help the blush that crept onto my cheeks. Things with David were easy. Or they had been. That was what I'd loved about it. That it was effortless. And yet…we'd royally fucked it up. All the complications had reared their ugly heads and shattered that illusion of simplicity.

"So…we should talk," I said.

"Your place or mine?"

I chewed on my bottom lip and weighed the pros and cons. Truthfully, neutral ground would be better, but at ten p.m., our options were pretty limited.

"Your place. Jen is watching Jason tonight at my place."

"All right. Meet you there?"

"Yeah."

David stopped and reached out to touch my arm. "It's just a talk, okay?"

I released the breath I'd been holding. Right. Just a talk. Nothing more. We could barely keep it together at the office. What was going to happen when I was at his house?

No, I wasn't going to think about that. I was going to drive over to his place. We were going to talk about why he never told me he was a Van Pelt. And then I was going to leave. Simple as that.

David's mansion was close to my house on the south side of town. He lived in the country club in an

The WRIGHT ONE

outrageous place all by himself. But, apparently, with the cost of living in San Francisco, he only would have been able to buy a shoebox there for the cost of this place. I guessed...the same would be true for New York City, too. The place he was really from.

I parked in the driveway, doubting my every move. Being here with him was not smart. Hearing him out was though.

I didn't want things to progress too quickly. I'd told the girls that I was willing to listen to David's side of the story. Maybe even give us the second chance that I never had with Maverick. But I didn't know what I was doing. And I didn't know if I was ready for that second chance.

But I had no choice right now. I would listen to what he had to say. Make any decisions from there.

I left the flowers in the car and hoped that the summer heat wouldn't ruin the buds. They were a sweet gesture. He'd looked so cute, standing at the front of the movie theater, holding them. Even if I hadn't intended for this to be a date. It *wasn't* a date.

Someone would believe that statement, I was sure...

David had already unlocked the front door, and I entered cautiously. He slipped off his jacket and slung it on the back of a barstool. He glanced down at his phone before depositing it on the island in the kitchen and sauntering back into the living room toward me. He looked delectable in a polo and shorts. I liked him in relaxed attire as much as a suit. But what really did me in was seeing him in his own element with the confidence that came with that.

He gestured to the couch. "Have a seat. Can I get you anything to drink?"

"Just water. Thanks."

"Don't mind if I have some bourbon, do you?"

"No." Though I was surprised.

"Good. This story…well, it needs something a little stronger."

I watched him pour a knuckle's worth of amber liquid into a glass and down it before pouring another. He brought it over along with my water and left them on coasters on the pristine glass coffee table.

What a contrast in our lives. A glass coffee table was one of the most ridiculous pieces of furniture you could have with a toddler in the house. It would always have fingerprints and Legos and juice and Cheerios and fifteen books and a smashed SpaghettiO or something. It would definitely never look like… this. #MomProblems

"I suppose I should start at the beginning." David took a seat in a chair across from me and sighed, as if this were going to be a long event.

"Wherever you want to start is fine."

"Bear with me." He took another sip of his bourbon. "When I was at Yale, I was getting a business degree so that, once I graduated, I could start working at the family company. I had every intention of taking over and running it when my father retired."

I swallowed. Oh God, I hoped I was ready for this.

"I was home for the summer and working for my father when I came across a string of suspicious emails that led to me finding out all of my parents' dark secrets. I'll spare you the boring details that you

The WRIGHT ONE

likely already know, but it was a long track record of dirty dealings and stolen money."

"Before that, you knew nothing?" I asked in disbelief.

"Did you know that your father had invested money with the Van Pelts before it went public?"

I shook my head. "I guess I didn't know much about the business as a child and had no interest when I grew up."

"Right. I was kind of a reluctant bystander in this. Destined to take over the company to make my petulant, irritable father proud of me. A man who couldn't even hug me, let alone treat me with affection. I'm not sure that I ever heard him tell me that he loved me."

David glanced away, lost in his own memory. I could tell that it still pained him to think about it all these years later. I hadn't had a great father, but he'd still doted on me. I knew that he loved me. I couldn't imagine growing up in world where I doubted my parent's affection.

"Anyway, I confronted my parents about what I'd discovered."

"That must have been difficult."

He laughed sardonically. "You have no idea. This was my legacy, and I was about to turn it upside down. But I was convinced it was a mistake, some error. That I was doing the right thing by bringing it to my parents' attention so that we could discuss it like adults."

I frowned at that. I'd always believed the Van Pelts were monsters, and David had worked under the impression for most of his life that they were the good guys. How had it hurt him to realize that he'd been played? It must have destroyed his sense of self to make him change his name and move to San Francisco.

"As you can imagine, it didn't go well. Obviously, it wasn't a lie, and I'd discovered years of careful manipulation and a decades-old Ponzi scheme. Instead of being rightfully horrified at what they'd done, they insisted that I couldn't tell anyone. Even made it seem like I was in on their secret club now that I knew."

My hand moved to my mouth in horror.

"But I couldn't take over a fake company. I felt cheated and lied to. I told them I was going to go to the police. That this wasn't right. They tried to tell me that no one would believe me, and then when I became more adamant, they told me they would disinherit me."

"Disinherit you? That's preposterous. They knew they'd lose everything. You'd have nothing to inherit anyway."

"Yeah, but at the time, it was a real threat. I was insane with anger, and throwing a disinheritance on top of it." He shook his head. "I completely lost it. I couldn't believe they'd do that to their only son."

"I can't believe anyone would say something that cruel to you when you were the one doing the right thing."

"They didn't think it was the right thing. They'd been doing this so long, they were blind."

"God, what fucking assholes," I said, jumping to my feet and burning with indignant rage against the Van Pelts all over again.

"They are," he agreed.

I ground my teeth together. No wonder he'd abandoned them. I couldn't even believe that Katherine had stayed on their side. That *anyone* could side with the Van Pelts. I felt validated. But, if he was so against the Van Pelts, then why the hell hadn't he told me? Of course we didn't like them, but I might have understood his own distaste for them; instead, he'd lied and proven he was more like them than he cared to admit.

"Sutton, please, sit down."

"Okay, okay." I plopped back on the couch and took a long drink of my water. "I just...I don't feel like this explains why you lied to me. If anything, I feel like this all would explain why you should have told me."

"I know." He steepled his fingers together and stared down at the bourbon in his almost-empty glass. "This isn't easy. I don't...I don't talk about these things. In fact, the only person who does know any of this is Katherine, and we don't see eye to eye. Confiding in people is hard from me. And, God, I just...I don't know how to say the next part."

I took a deep breath and then let it out. I was letting my fury get the best of me, and I needed to hear out the rest of his story. "Go ahead. I'm listening. I want to hear the rest."

"Well, when they said they'd disinherit me, I told them I couldn't believe that they'd do that to their only son." His eyes moved up to mine. "And my father said...that I wasn't his son."

Eight

David

"Excuse me?" Sutton asked.

Her eyes were round with confusion and disbelief. The look I'd been expecting from her. The look I expected from everyone. That was why I had never told this story.

"Like...what does that mean? Did your mom...have an affair? Are you not actually your dad's son...like biologically? Why would he raise you as his son if you weren't?" she blurted out. "I'm sorry. I have so many questions."

"I'd be more surprised if you didn't." I finished off my drink and then continued, "No, she didn't have an affair. As far as I know at least. No affair that resulted in me. I was adopted."

Sutton furrowed her brows. "But...why? Like, they had every option available to them. IVF and fertility treatments and all that."

"When she was younger than you, my mom was told that she could never have kids. They always planned to adopt."

"So, is Katherine adopted, too?"

"No," I said on a sigh. "Katherine is theirs. My mother had her thyroid removed shortly after I was adopted. There was a history of thyroid cancer in her family, and after she went through treatments, ta-da, Katherine."

"Wow." Sutton blinked a ton. "Wow."

"Yeah, she was their miracle baby while I was…this abomination they'd purchased."

"David," she whispered sadly.

"Okay. That's not true." It felt true sometimes. But it was more likely that my father was just a total dick. "I was angry, and I told them that I'd rather be no one than their son. I left their place, changed my name, and found out where my biological parents lived, and as soon as I graduated college, I upped and moved to San Francisco."

"Ohhh," Sutton muttered. "Your biological parents live in San Francisco."

"Yes. So, every time you asked if my parents lived there…I said yes. Because they do."

"But not the ones who raised you."

I shook my head. "No, not the ones who raised me. But I didn't know how to tell you that. I've never told anyone that."

"Not even Katherine?"

"No. I was in San Francisco when the story broke about my parents."

"So, you never told on them?"

The WRIGHT ONE

I glanced down at the empty glass in my hands. "No. Despite all my bluster, I chose to walk instead of doing something."

She was silent for a long time. I felt her judgment weighing on me. But I already felt shitty about it. In the end, I'd sided with them. I could have turned them in and gone traitor on my own parents, but I hadn't done it. They'd made a misstep that someone else turned them in for. It was wrong of me not to incriminate them, but at the end of the day, I hadn't been able to do it. I'd wanted to start over rather than wade deeper into their shit.

"Once the truth came out, my parents told Katherine about where I was and that I'd changed my name. She came looking for me because she wanted me on their side."

"But why? How could she side with them?"

"She's loyal to a fault. She would never turn her back on someone she cared about. Even if she had to be dragged through the mud with them."

Sutton sighed and seemed to contemplate that. She had to understand that quality. The Wrights had it in spades.

"I stayed out of the media when the story broke and stayed in San Francisco—building an empire and meeting my new family. I thought no one could be worse than my old family. Fuck, they were all over the news. They were atrocious scumbag liars. But, still...I was wrong."

"Your biological family was worse than the Van Pelts?" she asked in disbelief.

"In a different way, but yes. They didn't know I was a Van Pelt. It was a closed adoption. The Van Pelts didn't want my biological parents to come looking for a payout when they realized who had adopted me. And that was good for me for a long time. My bio parents greeted me with open arms. I helped them move into a new house in Silicon Valley. I met their children…my real siblings. They were all married with multiple kids, and I suddenly had this giant family with nieces and nephews and everything. The love and support I'd always dreamed of."

"Like what you see with my family."

"Yes," I told her. "But it was a lie. They skimmed money from me for years for drugs and alcohol. When they found out I was a Van Pelt, they tried to gain access to my trust fund. Then, when that failed, they blackmailed me, saying that they would go to the media and out me as David Van Pelt if I didn't help fund their heroin habits."

"Shit," Sutton gasped.

"I gave them enough money to shut up, applied to every job known to man to get out…"

"And moved here," she finished for me.

I nodded. "Yes. The middle of nowhere. A new start where hopefully neither of my families could ever bother me again. Fuck, how wrong I was."

Sutton ran a hand back through her brown-to-blonde hair and then took another long sip of water. "You're right. This story *does* need something stronger."

"Bourbon?" I offered.

"Maybe just a bit."

We both wandered into the kitchen where I poured her a drink. She took a shot of liquid courage. I could see her mind whirring to life. As if everything that I'd said was sinking in.

And it felt...nice. I hadn't known how it would feel to finally say all of that out loud. For someone else to know all that I had endured. The shitty families and the lies and fraud and drugs. How no one had ever really loved me. Except maybe Holli...and even she had committed suicide rather than stay in this world with me.

But, either way, it felt like a weight off my shoulders. Now, Sutton knew everything. Finally, she knew it all, and she could judge for herself whether or not I was worthy of her anger. My name alone could wreck me one more time, and if it did, I didn't know if I'd recover from it again.

"So...you're not actually a Van Pelt. You're a Calloway. I'm assuming your real parents' last name is Calloway?"

I nodded. "It is. But I suppose I'm both. I was raised by the Van Pelts. I only spent a few short years with my biological family. I'm thankful that my mom and dad adopted me. It was the best thing for me. I would never have been raised the way I was. I would never have gone to Yale. I probably wouldn't even be here right now. I can't fault them for the life that they gave me."

"Right," she said. "I can't imagine giving up a child though."

"It took a long time for me to come to terms with it."

"And this is...everything? There aren't any more surprises lurking?"

"Uh, no," I said with a laugh. "I think this is enough."

"No, you're right. It's a lot. I get why you kept it from me. I'd imagine it's difficult to talk about."

"It is."

"I can understand not wanting to be part of your family. I love my family, but it's not always easy to be a Wright."

"Families are all assholes," I told her.

"Thank you for telling me. It's not an excuse for not confiding in me before, but it's a reason. A pretty damn good one at that."

"So...where does that leave us?" I prompted.

Sutton didn't say anything for a minute. She poured herself another drink and then let it flow down her throat before looking back up at me. But what I saw stunned me. There was no awkwardness or uncertainty in that gaze. There might be a touch of wariness, but I saw real warmth. True concern. And...something like hope.

Then, without a word, she stood up on her tiptoes and pressed her lips against mine. I leaned into that embrace, wrapping my arms around her waist and tugging her closer against me. Her lips were electric, and our kiss was charged with energy. This was nothing like the first time we'd kissed. Nothing hesitant or questioning in it. Just pure desire.

Her hands moved to the front of my shorts, and she ran her fingers along the hem. I jerked against her teasing touch. Then she flicked the button on my shorts.

I pulled back from her and was about to open my mouth to question her, but she smiled and said, "This is what it means for us."

Well, I was on board. This seemed too good to be true. Having her here again, in my arms. I'd promised to fight for her, but I hadn't been sure that she would come around. I knew this wasn't the end of our discussion, but at least, it was a chance.

She tugged me back down to her lips. I ran my tongue along her bottom lip until she opened herself to me. Then, our tongues touched, tasted, tempted. Until I couldn't hold back any longer. I wanted all of her. I'd fucking missed her this last week. And I felt like an ass for making her go through this.

My hand slipped up the front of her yellow tank top and stopped abruptly when I realized that she wasn't wearing a bra. Fuck. My dick hardened painfully in my shorts, and I pressed harder against her. I continued moving higher until I caressed the underside of her breast and traced the outline. Her body responded in kind, rubbing against my dick and moving her hand down my boxers. I cupped her breast and flicked my thumb across her nipple.

Our lips broke apart, her head tilted back, and she moaned. As she was distracted, her finger brushed against the head of my cock, causing me to groan at her touch. We were both starved for contact.

When she looked at me again, her pupils were dilated, and she had a devious smile on her lips. She dragged her shirt over her head, tossing it onto the tiled floor. Then, she made quick work of my shorts and boxers. Her eyes rounded at the sight of my cock before she took the length of it in her small hand.

"God, I fucking missed you," I growled as she stroked me up and down a few times.

"Show me how much," she said.

I popped the button on her shorts and tugged them off, thong and all. Then, I hoisted her into the air. She gasped, throwing her legs around my waist. I jerked her backward against the refrigerator door. Her body smacked against the stainless steel. Her arms banded around my neck, and she dragged her bottom lip into her mouth.

"This much," I told her.

Then, I grabbed her very fine ass in both of my hands and slowly lowered her onto my cock.

"Oh God," she moaned.

I was so glad that she was on the pill right now.

I didn't move until her wet pussy was wrapped fully around me. Her walls clenched as I filled her completely. Then, I anchored her against the fridge and slammed back into her. She cried out, a smile breaking onto her face. And I did it again. And again. And again.

Our bodies crashed together like waves on the beach. Pulled out by the tide and then crashed back together time and time again.

"Fuck," she mumbled. "Oh fuck, I'm going to come."

I increased the tempo, meeting her fevered gasps and entering her tight womb. We reached a peak when I felt her muscles contract all around me. I did nothing to stifle her screams of pleasure as she came hard on my cock, milking every last drop of cum from me.

She leaned her head back and panted. Her chest rising and falling rapidly. My head fell forward onto her shoulder as I finished. Then, with a sigh, I pulled out of her and let her feet hit the kitchen floor.

"I think…we have a thing for kitchens," she said. She held on to the refrigerator door as her legs wobbled.

"I will fuck you anytime you want in any kitchen. Just say the word."

THE WRIGHT ONE

She laughed. "God, I don't know if I can walk."

"I like that."

"You're bad."

I pulled her close again and kissed her hard on the mouth. "Come to New York with me."

"What?" she gasped.

"You want to know me. You want to know my life. I'll take you to the city. I'll show you my life. It's not pretty, but New York is."

"You're serious?" Her eyes scanned my face for a hint of deception, but there was none.

"Absolutely."

She nodded slowly. "Okay."

"I haven't been back in a few years, so I can't guarantee that it's going to be…pleasant."

She pressed a finger to my lips. "I'll be with you, and you'll be showing yourself to me. That's good enough for me."

Nine

Sutton

My head was in the clouds by the time I made it home that night. I'd gone to the movie, hesitant but hopeful. And it had ended…well, amazingly. I still had a lot to think about regarding his parents and the adoption and everything. It was so much to take in. But it also explained so much about him. I was excited that he was going to share New York with me, too. That we were going to get back on the same playing field.

I strolled into my house and found Jenny passed out on the couch. I gently shook her shoulder. "Hey, sleepyhead."

Jen rubbed her eyes and sat up. "Sorry. I didn't mean to fall asleep."

"It's okay. It's kind of late."

"Have a good night?" she asked. Then, she grinned when she saw the state of my attire. "A really good night?"

I laughed and ran a shaky hand through my disheveled hair. "Yeah. It went better than expected."

"Good. I'm glad you went."

"Me, too."

Jenny stretched and then stood. "I'm going to head out. I'll see you on Monday."

"Sounds good." Jen headed for the door when I remembered about New York. "Hey! Are you by any chance free to watch Jason next weekend? David wants to take me out of town."

"Oh crap, you know I would, but that's my big PCAT testing weekend. Intense classes and two fully timed tests."

"Right. I forgot that was next weekend."

"Yeah. I'm kind of a wreck. I don't even know if I'm ready for this."

"You'll do great."

"Thanks." She smiled. "I hope you find someone for Jason. Wish I could help."

"No, you're awesome. You're always a help. I don't know what I'm going to do without you."

"You're a great mom, Sut. You'll make it work."

I locked the door behind Jenny and then hurried down the hall to Jason's room. His door was cracked open with a night-light near the floor. I eased inside on silent feet, brushed his hair off his forehead, and then planted a kiss on his cheek.

"Love you, little man."

I tucked him in and then reluctantly headed to my room with the big king-size bed. It felt strangely large and empty. I never shared this bed with a man other than Maverick, but tonight…I really wished David were here.

The WRIGHT ONE

Jason and I passed the weekend in a whirlwind of activities that ended in exhaustion. I had no idea how that kid had such limitless energy. I felt ragged by the time I made it into the bakery Monday morning, bright and early. Luckily, baking brought out the best in me, and I perked up after my first rather large thermos of coffee.

Kimber was already hard at work, making a fresh batch of chocolate cupcakes, when I threw my apron on and entered the back.

"Morning," she said.

"Good morning," I said. "Smells heavenly."

"Will you check the far oven? The vanilla should be ready."

I put on oven mitts and removed the perfectly fluffy cupcakes from the oven. I left them to cool and then moved into step with Kimber. We worked for an hour or two in quiet conversation before the morning cashier, Mary Elizabeth, arrived to help with final touches.

"Okay. I can finish the rest up here if you want to head up front," Kimber told us.

"Sounds good," Mary Elizabeth said.

Before I left, I turned back to Kimber. "Hey, is there any chance you could take Jason for the weekend? David wants to take me out of town."

"Oh, are you two back together?" she asked, her interest piqued.

"We're working on it. Trying to be open to second chances."

"I'm glad. I like him." Then, she frowned. "But I actually think this weekend is bad for me. It's the weekend before Emery's wedding, and we have so much stuff left to do. Plus, the boys are all leaving for the bachelor party. Thank God the bachelorette thing was a couple of weeks ago."

"Yeah, I'm glad she wanted to have it before school started for her."

Emery was a high school teacher.

"Same. So, I think that I'll be too busy. I'm sorry."

"No, I totally get it. This is so last minute!"

"Well, let me know if you can't get it to work. I could try if no one else is free."

"Don't worry about it. This is like a Hail Mary. If we don't get to go, it won't be the end of the world. Just thought I'd try."

"Okay. Are you sure?"

I nodded. "Yes. Thank you for even considering it."

"Well, I love you and that boy," Kimber said, pulling me into a flour-filled hug.

"I love you, too, and I'm so glad to be working here."

"You're a godsend, honestly. We should probably send you to school to learn to be a pastry chef; you're so brilliant."

I blushed. "Do you think I need more schooling?"

"Need? That's relative. I think you're smart enough to do it."

"Thank you, Kimber."

I smiled all the way back up to the front and for the rest of the day as I considered culinary school for the first time. My best friend was starting medical school. My other best friend/nanny was working on her dream to become a pharmacist. Why *shouldn't* I try to become a pastry chef?

It was a thought. One I would have after I figured out how I was going to get away this weekend.

I was pretty sure that bringing Jason along just…wasn't exactly an option. Not for the kind of weekend I wanted to have with David.

I mulled over it on my way home, and I was parked at a red light, fixing my hair in the rearview mirror, when an idea hit me over the head.

"Well, shit," I grumbled as I realized what I had to do.

I heaved a sigh and then carefully drove the exact speed limit the rest of the way home. I wanted to speed, but that damn speeding ticket was still irritating me. As soon as I showed up, Jen disappeared to study, and once she was gone, I bundled Jason back into the car.

"Where are we going, Mommy?" Jason asked from his car seat in the back.

"We're going to visit Grandma and Grandpa. Are you excited?"

"Yay!" he cheered.

His favorite Disney songs played through the radio on the way out of Lubbock and into the boonies. Maverick's parents, Linda and Ray, lived on a farm about twenty minutes outside of town. I'd found it endearing when we were together, but it also was never a possibility that I was going to live that life.

In some respects, I was more like David than I ever knew. I was as much a Wright through and through as he was a Van Pelt. Even if he was adopted, it was still who he was...just like it was who I was.

Maverick had been that beacon of goodness that I loved for so long. That one person who hadn't just seen Wright when he looked at me. But he also hadn't understood the pressure either. He hadn't gotten that I had my own difficulties with being who I was.

And it wasn't until I was driving back onto that damn farm that I realized...I needed that, too. It was refreshing that David and I shared that. We shared something that Maverick and I never had, which was a relief. Not a comparison, just a different person, and I liked that. That feeling of new.

My tires rumbled over the gravel road that led to the charming red brick house. It had been built on a cotton farm as far as the eye could see. Maverick had loved this place. It made me feel guilty that I didn't bring Jason more often. But I was doing it now, and that was all that mattered. Even if I had ulterior motives.

I helped Jason out of the car seat, grabbed his bag, and followed him up to the front door. I knocked once, but the front door swung open at the slightest touch.

"Jason!" Linda cried. She bent down and scooped him up into her arms. "What a pleasant surprise. How are you?"

"Good, Grandma."

"Come in, come in." She gestured for me to follow. "So good to see you, Sutton. It's never often enough. I'm so glad that you brought him by."

"Grandpa!" Jason said and then rushed for his grandpa.

Ray wrapped his arms around Jason.

The WRIGHT ONE

"Trucks?"

"Yes, of course! Let's go out back and look at the trucks. If you're lucky, I might even put you up in the tractor."

"Be careful!" I warned.

Ray waved his hand at me. "We'll be fine. Get a drink and relax."

I laughed at his easy demeanor and followed Linda into the living room.

"Sweet tea?"

"Please."

She returned a minute later with two glasses of sweet tea and some snickerdoodle cookies on a tray. She placed it on the coffee table.

"We are so happy to have you and Jason here with us. What's the occasion?"

"I thought you'd want to see your grandson."

Linda reached out and clasped my hand. "We're happy to see you, too. You're like a daughter to us."

I smiled warmly, basking in the glow of affection. Sometimes, I forgot what it was like to have parental figures in my life. I hadn't really grown up with them other than Jensen, and despite everything he'd done, he was still just my brother.

"Thank you. I was also wondering if you could keep Jason for the weekend. I know that he'd love to spend a weekend with y'all."

"Trying to get some time to yourself?"

I took a deep breath and went for it. "I have plans to go out of town, and I'll be back on Sunday, if that would be all right."

"Where are you going?"

"New York," I confessed.

"Oh! Quite some way. I've never been to New York. Why aren't you taking Jason? I bet he'd love the skyscrapers."

"I think he would love it but likely not remember it. I'm going to take him when he's older."

"Who are you taking instead?"

She was fishing, and I knew that I had to tell her. *Here goes nothing.*

"David."

"Ah, the infamous David. Do you think it's a wise decision to travel with him so soon?"

"Please, don't do this."

"Do what? Worry for you?"

"I still love Maverick. But I need this, okay? I don't want us to be at odds about this. David is a part of my life, and I've made my decision to give us a chance."

"How does Jason feel about this?" she asked, reaching for her sweet tea.

"Linda, please, I take Jason into consideration, but even if he had a thought about my love life, I would not let him make my decisions for me. He's two. He's a happy, growing boy. I don't bring David around him, except at events, and we're careful not to show affection. I put him first in everything, but I can't dictate my love life based on him, okay?"

Linda held up her hand. "I wasn't trying to make you feel bad. I was just asking."

"You're never just asking."

Linda grinned. "I worry. I don't have a son to worry over, so I do it for you and Jason now. If you're happy and Jason is happy, that's what matters."

I released a breath. "Thank you. It means a lot to hear you say that."

"Just be careful, okay? With your heart and your son's heart. I couldn't bear to see either of them broken again."

"Thank you."

"Anytime you need us to watch Jason, just give us a holler. We're more than happy to have him." Linda rose to her feet. "Now, let's go outside and see my grandson drive a tractor fourteen years before he gets a license."

I laughed but followed her outside. I'd thought this was going to be harder. Last time I'd talked to them about David, Linda had completely freaked out on me. I'd worried it would be like that again. But I hadn't let her prey on my insecurities. I felt stronger. It was a relief, and I felt lucky to have them in my life.

Ten

David

We touched down at JFK International Airport early Friday afternoon. When I'd invited Sutton to come to New York with me, I'd been in the throes of passion. Or maybe I'd hit my head too hard. Because, now that I was here, I was not at all as confident as I'd felt when I had her back against that refrigerator.

It had been years since I was in my hometown, and I was not the man I'd been when I left. The day I'd turned my back on this place was the day that everything changed. For the better. I'd forgotten how suffocating this life was, and it took only two minutes after walking out into the smoggy summer air to remember.

Our chauffeur appeared then in a slick black Mercedes. He opened the back door for us and stowed our luggage, and then we were off.

Sutton yawned. "I'm going to need a nap. Jason had me up all last night. He was so excited about staying at his grandparents' that he refused to sleep."

"He's lucky to have them in his life. Even if that makes you tired."

"True. I'm glad they agreed to watch him, especially since the last time we talked it didn't go so well."

I understood Maverick's parents' unease. They'd lost a son, and now, the only two people who understood their grief were moving on. Or I was sure that was how they saw it. But I wasn't replacing Maverick in anyone's life. I wanted my own place in Sutton's and Jason's lives.

"Me, too." I leaned over and kissed her forehead. "Why don't you try to rest? With the traffic, it'll probably be an hour until we get into Manhattan."

"Nah. I'm pretty used to the exhaustion."

She had said that and then promptly fell asleep against the window a few minutes later. I laughed softly under my breath and then watched my city come into focus.

Manhattan was a bustling metropolis of skyscrapers and chaotic streets and noise. So much noise. We crossed the bridge onto the island, and all the sights and sounds and smells assaulted me. Something settled in my chest. A feeling of rightness. I hadn't known how much I missed it.

I'd forced myself to stay away. But, now that I was here, even the suffocating aspects of the Upper East Side didn't seem so bad. I'd probably feel differently once I had to deal with it all again. Right now, I'd revel in that rightness. Knowing it wouldn't last long.

The WRIGHT ONE

I shook Sutton awake when we arrived.

"Oh God, sorry." She rubbed her eyes and blearily looked up at me. "Did I pass out?"

"You did. We're here. You ready?"

"Yeah, I'm alive." She slunk out of the backseat, and I watched as her mouth popped open. "We're staying at The Plaza?"

"I said I'd show you my world." I walked around to her side of the car and wrapped an arm around her waist.

It was kind of cute to see her like this. Sutton Wright, who had a trust fund and a family name with more money than God, being awed by me taking her to The Plaza. Lubbock and New York might as well have been on different continents.

"Good," she said with a smile on her face.

I checked us in up front before we took the elevator up to the top floor. I might have gone overboard when I'd promised Sutton I'd show her my life. I hadn't lived liked this in a long time, but expensive taste had never left me. It was why I had the Ferrari and basically a mansion. You could take the boy out of the Upper East Side, but you couldn't take the Upper East Side out of the boy.

"Well then," Sutton said, dropping her bag in the front room. She arched an eyebrow. "Now, you're just showing off."

I laughed. "Only the best for my girl."

"If you think a penthouse suite is going to get me on your good side, then...you're absolutely right."

"You're ridiculous," I said, dragging her into a kiss.

"Let me find one of the bedrooms. There has to be at least three in this place," she teased against my lips. "Then, we can see who's ridiculous."

I groaned and leaned my forehead against hers. "Hold that thought. We have plans."

"Oh? I thought we were just here to have a lot of make-up sex."

"That, too."

"Going to clue me in?"

"We're going to Central Park."

"And tell me again how we can't do that after hot, sweaty make-up sex?"

"You're killing me," I groaned.

"I could in the best way." Her hand moved down the front of my pants.

"Going to have to stop you there and promise to seduce you heavily tonight. But…we have to go meet my sister."

She yanked her hand out of my pants. "What a buzzkill."

"I'm the worst."

"*The* Katherine Van Pelt?" She chewed on her lip. "I'm glad you didn't give me much time to be nervous."

"Oh, there's still plenty of time."

She smacked my arm. "Not helping. I have to change into something presentable."

"I think you look beautiful."

"Suck-up," she called as she investigated the rest of the penthouse to find the bedroom.

It took her another twenty minutes before she emerged from the bathroom. Her hair had fresh waves in them, her makeup had been touched up, and she'd changed out of her traveling clothes and into a pale blue sundress and Tory Burch sandals. "Okay?"

"I'm reconsidering leaving."

She winked. "Maybe later if you're lucky."

"I'm lucky."

Every step that we took away from The Plaza and into Central Park felt like a step closer to my undoing. I'd told Katherine that we were coming into town. I'd assured her that she would get to meet Sutton but only if she promised not to bring up any of the shit with our parents. I didn't want to hear a word of her propaganda. It was uncomfortable enough for me. Would be even more so for Sutton, who had only just found out I was a Van Pelt and had been managing her hatred of them for almost a decade.

I loved Katherine. She was loyal, considerate, passionate, and someone you always wanted in your corner. But she was also vapid, nosy, pretentious, and condescending. That was who they had made her. That was who I would have been if not for Holli saving me from the bullshit. When Katherine liked you, it was the best place in the world. When she didn't, you might as well not exist.

"You seem more nervous than I do," Sutton said.

We strolled hand in hand down the tree-lined walkway. It was a hot afternoon, and the trees were keeping the sun at bay.

"It's been a while since I've seen her."

She squeezed my hand. "It'll be fine."

Sutton was reassuring me about meeting someone who, up until two weeks ago, she had utterly despised on principle. God, this woman was perfect for me.

We continued down Central Park Mall, past all the famous benches, and down the stairs that led to Bethesda Fountain. There, standing at the base of the fountain, stood my sister. Her face was buried in her phone, but it was unmistakably her in a designer dress and heels, looking like she'd just stepped off a runway.

"Whoa," Sutton muttered under her breath.

"Yeah." We moved over to where Katherine was standing, and I cleared my throat. "Katherine."

Her head popped up, and a smile graced her features. "Oh my God, David!"

Then, she threw all pretense aside and launched into my arms. I laughed, disarmed by her fervor. The Katherine I knew never hugged, especially not in public. She was an air-kiss-only kind of person.

"It's so good to see you," she gushed. She disentangled herself and ran a manicured hand back through her long, dark hair.

"You, too." I gestured to Sutton. "Sutton, my sister, Katherine. Ren, this is Sutton."

"Pleasure to meet you," Katherine said, leaning forward and air-kissing Sutton's cheeks.

"You, too," Sutton said. "I've heard so much about you."

Katherine arched an eyebrow. "I'm sure they're all lies."

Sutton laughed. "It was all good things."

"Oh," Katherine said with a careless grin. "Then, I'm sure it's all true."

𝒯𝒽𝑒 WRIGHT ONE

She linked arms with Sutton and walked her over to the edge of the lake, carefully avoiding all tourists.

"How was the flight? Easy trip? Have you been to New York before? Are you enjoying yourself so far?" Katherine asked.

"Easy on the interrogation mode, Ren," I told her.

"I'm just excited. It's not every day my brother is in the city, let alone with his girlfriend. I've never even met one of your girlfriends before. You're going to have to give me this one, David."

"I don't mind," Sutton said. "I'm excited to meet you, too. And, yes, it was an easy flight, but no, not my first time in New York. I've been a bunch. My brother used to live here for a while."

"Jensen, right?" Katherine asked.

"Yeah."

Katherine tapped her lip. "I do remember him. He's friends with Penn."

"Yes, I recently discovered that as well."

"I thought he was hot. Too bad he was married. At least he's single now."

Sutton laughed. "His wedding is next weekend actually."

"Damn! Missed my chance again."

"Aren't you engaged?" Sutton asked with a raised eyebrow.

"Yeah, Ren, aren't you engaged?" I goaded.

"I am. You'll meet Camden tomorrow," Katherine said, losing all warmth from her tone at the mention of her fiancé.

Sutton glanced over at me with a question in her eyes. I'd have to explain that whole situation to her tonight. Because Camden Percy was not a train wreck you wanted to walk into, unprepared.

"Wait, what do you mean, tomorrow?" I asked.

Katherine gave me a simpering look. "There's an event tomorrow at the MET. I got you two tickets when I found out you were coming."

"Ren," I groaned.

"It'll be fun. Plus, it will give Sutton and me girl time tomorrow at the spa."

"Spa?" Sutton asked with raised eyebrows.

"I booked us with my specialist. You'll love him." Katherine touched Sutton's arm and then winked at me. "Don't worry. I promise to steal her for only an hour or three."

"Why am I not surprised?" I grumbled.

But Sutton looked as if she was interested in the notion. It wasn't *my* idea of spending time together in New York, but Katherine was putting in the effort. I could give her that. I just had a bad feeling about going to a MET event. Katherine was a socialite. That was basically her job. Sutton and I didn't belong in this world, and I knew how they treated outsiders.

"It'll be fun," Katherine said, nudging me. "Don't look so dour."

"I'm game if Sutton is."

"You did say you wanted to show me your life," she said, throwing my words back at me.

I sure hoped I didn't regret them.

Eleven

Sutton

"So, what do you think of my sister?" David asked when we finally made it back to the hotel later that day.

I was utterly exhausted. I really had not had enough sleep last night.

We'd spent an exorbitant amount of time eating at Tavern on the Green before Katherine had to disappear to some meeting. I still didn't understand what she did exactly, but she made it seem important.

My eyes were wide when I looked up at David. "She's a lot but in a good way."

David laughed heartily before sinking into an oversize chair in the sitting area. "That's the nicest way I've ever heard someone describe her."

"That can't be true. She was genuinely happy to see you, and she treated me well. She's taking me to the spa tomorrow. I think she seems like a girl with the world on her shoulders, pretending like she's on top of the world."

"Also accurate," he agreed.

"What do you think about her? Is she different to you?"

"In some ways. In other ways, she's exactly the same."

"I'm surprised she never brought up your parents."

"I asked her not to."

"Oh. Aren't you interested in seeing them since you're here?"

He shook his head. "Not in the least."

I frowned and considered that. I hated what the Van Pelts had done to my family and how they had treated David. I hated that the very mention of that name had pushed us apart. Or that I'd had to second-guess our relationship when he was nothing but genuine in all other regards. He cared for me and Jason and the company. He was understanding, loyal, gentle, and constant. He drew out passion in me that I hadn't felt in over a year. But he was still hurting, and that was obvious to me.

"I think, if my parents were still here, I'd want to see them even if they'd done wrong. Maybe they've changed?"

"Are you defending my parents?"

"No. Absolutely not. I despise them for all they've done to hurt you and me and us. But...they're still your parents. It'd be a shame not to see them while you're here."

"Well, this trip is for us," David said, pulling me down onto his lap. "So, maybe I'll do it on another trip."

The WRIGHT ONE

"I don't believe you." I straddled his lap and ran my hands up his chest and around his neck.

"I said I wouldn't lie to you."

"Another trip could be anytime in the future."

"All I'm thinking about is our future."

"Oh?" I asked with a small smile.

"Like how we're going to break in that bed."

"And here I thought, you were being romantic when you were actually being filthy."

He laughed. "You like that though. I heard your moans when I threw you against the fridge."

My cheeks heated at the statement, and I ground my hips against his. "That is true."

"But, if you want to hear me tell you that, by our future, I'm thinking about spending time with you and your boy, being the man you want and deserve, having a life of our own, then yes, I think about that future, too."

My heart thundered in my chest so hard, it was ringing in my ears. "You really think about that?"

"Would I have brought you here if I didn't want you in every part of my life?" His hands trailed up my neck to cup my face and ease my lips down onto his. Our eyes locked in the small space leftover after the kiss. "I have wanted you since the first day I saw you sprawled out on a blanket with Jason on the Fourth of July. I didn't know anything about you. I didn't know anything that would follow. I just knew that you glowed with an unparalleled energy. You were radiant. Unequivocally stunning, even in the simplicity of the situation. Maybe because of it." He ran his thumb across my bottom lip. "I spent a year waiting for you to regain your joy, and I feel lucky just to be a part of your life."

I was stunned into silence at his declaration.

He'd felt all of this for me for so long while I was stuck in my own slice of hell. Everyone had seen his affection but me. I'd brushed it off as a new friendship, unable to see what was really happening.

David was the one who had helped me all those months I was dead inside. All those times I needed a sitter for Jason, just to escape. All those times I heard ghosts in my house and voices that woke me in the night, expecting Maverick, his absence overwhelming me.

David had been a beacon in the darkness.

He had been the shining light that kept me from sinking to the bottom of the ocean and drowning in my own grief.

It had taken me a year to realize that we were right for each other.

To accept that I could feel this again.

To trust in love once more.

We might have been on rocky ground, but being here with him, when I knew how much strength it had taken to get to this moment, just proved that I had made the right decision. My feelings for David had never wavered. Just my uncertainty about his own feelings.

My heart had always been in the right place. But was his?

Staring down at him in a penthouse suite in New York City, it had never been clearer that the answer was yes. Beyond yes. He'd had those feelings a year before I could admit my own.

His secrets were armor. Bulletproof and impenetrable. Weathered from years of battle.

But I'd removed each piece until all that was left was my David. The man before me. And it felt right. *We* felt right.

"Sutton," he whispered. There was unease in his voice, as if he was worried he'd just lost me.

"Thank you for being my joy when I needed it most," I told him.

A smile grew on his face. Then, he captured my lips and stood. My legs wrapped tight around his waist as he scooped me up and strode into the bedroom.

Our lips were unhurried as they moved against each other.

This wasn't the feverish make-up sex we'd had last week.

This was a claiming, a promise.

He set me on my feet at the edge of the bed. His hazel eyes were like honey in the dim lighting, and his affections were just as smooth. With gentle care, he slipped his hands down my arms and over my waist before dropping to his knees before me. I exhaled on a hiss as he moved both hands up my calves and over my sensitive inner thighs. Then, he nudged my feet further apart.

My inner walls clenched as he pushed me a little bit wider. His gaze found mine just as he reached the edge of my bubblegum-pink thong. He slipped one finger under the material and ran it around the edges from top to bottom, stopping right before he reached the place I really wanted him. I tried to push him back toward my opening, but he ignored my attempt. Apparently, he was going to take his time. I'd be lying if I said I wasn't a willing participant. I desperately wanted him to go fast, fast, fast, but slow, so slow, was making me soak through my thong.

His finger hooked into the top of the material and drew them down my legs. I stepped out of them at his insistence. He casually tossed them behind himself before moving back between my legs. One hand moved to grasp my ass while his other made the journey back up my inner thighs.

I groaned with impatience and need. He was teasing me, and I fucking loved it. And wanted it over. Fuck, I wanted to yield control to him, and at the same time, I wanted to throw him down on the floor and fuck his brains out.

Then, one finger slipped between my folds and found out just how wet I was from his ministrations.

"Mmm," he said approvingly, slicking his finger before moving to my clit and stroking me in circles.

I couldn't even buck or move out of his embrace with the way he held me captive. I could only stand there, legs wide, as he stroked my clit until I was gasping for breath. I was close. So fucking close. I could have tipped over the edge just from him playing with my clit, but as I felt my walls contracting, he pulled back.

"No!" I gasped.

He laughed, coming to his feet, still fully fucking clothed. "Take your dress off and lie on your back." He tugged his shirt off, and then as I started to crawl onto the bed, he amended, "Legs spread."

I flushed at his command, but I was ready to touch myself to get off at this point, so I did as I had been told. I'd pay him back later. A flush crept onto my cheeks as I lay back on the bed, opened my legs before him, and sat there and watched him strip out of his clothes. Slowly. One fucking piece at a time.

Then, when he was fully undressed, his cock jutting toward me, he grasped my hips in his hands and jerked me to the end of the bed. I squeaked in surprise. My ass was nearly hanging off the edge. My fingers dug into the comforter for support. And my body was begging for everything he was going to give me.

To my shock, he sank back onto his knees, and before I could utter a word, he buried his face between my legs. His tongue laved across my clit, alternating between flicking and sucking. I started to close my legs as my climax approached again. But he was having none of that. My heart stuttered and body throbbed in pleasure as he forced my legs open wider.

"Oh God," I groaned. "Please let me come. Dear fucking God, I'm begging you, David."

His fingers trailed down my thigh and then to the opening of my pussy. He inserted two inside me, curving them as he pulled them back out. It took three strokes of his fingers while his mouth was on my clit before I came in a sea of starlight. My vision going dark and then blasting out into the heavens. My entire body convulsed. My heart galloped ahead of me.

The next thing I heard was screaming. And I realized it was me.

My legs dropped to the sides, trembling. My eyes gradually opened, half-lidded and sex-drunk. I could still feel my heart beating in my abdomen.

"My…my turn," I offered, dazed.

"Oh no, Sut," he said with a lazy smile. "Making you come multiple times tonight is my pleasure."

I laughed deliriously. "Where did you come from?"

He leaned over me, resting his elbows on either side of my body. "You're in my city. This is where I came from. But you're home."

Then, with a gentleness my still-pulsing center needed, he drove forward into me. I moaned, and he smothered it with a kiss. I wrapped my arms and legs tight around his body, keeping him close so that we were pressed together as one. He started up a steady rhythm.

Touching every part of me.

My body.

My heart.

My soul.

He filled me to bursting. Giving as much as he was getting. Taking as much as I was offering.

The moment felt final.

Not an ending, but a beginning.

An understanding that there was no going back from here.

He released my lips to look down on me as he picked up the pace. Our bodies were flushed and warm. My heart full. And I saw everything he'd ever felt, everything he'd ever wanted to say to me, *everything* in his eyes. They were windows to the devotion he was showing me. To the person he'd become to be with me. To the openness he'd never had with anyone else.

And I was starting anew.

No longer defined by what I'd lost.

But what I had gained.

And, when we finished together, lost to our passion, I felt truly whole once more.

Twelve

Sutton

I had been nervous about spending three full hours alone with Katherine at the spa the next day, but it was actually wonderful. David had had to be exaggerating about his sister. She clearly lived a different life than my own. When she'd discovered I worked at a bakery, she'd been completely flummoxed. I could tell that she was feeling me out, trying to figure out who I was and where I fit in to David's life. Not that I blamed her. I did the same thing to each of my brother's girlfriends. But I actually was shocked to say that I liked her.

That was even more surprising, considering she was a Van Pelt. I'd been certain I'd hate all of them. Now, here I was in a floor-length dress, going to a gala event with them. What a topsy-turvy world.

"Stop fidgeting," Katherine said, rapping my hand in the backseat. "He's going to go crazy when he sees you."

I dropped my hands to the sides and smiled at Katherine. "Are we going to pick up Camden, too?"

She frowned. "No. We're meeting him at the MET."

I arched an eyebrow in her direction. I was interested in meeting Katherine's fiancé. David had told me that he was a bit of a jackass from his limited experience with him. But Katherine's clear distaste made no sense. Why marry a guy you clearly hated?

"Oh, there he is! Hop out, so he can see the dress," Katherine said, all but pushing me out of the limo.

I laughed back at her as I stumbled forward, careful not to stick my heel into the back of the dress. It had been a while since I wore anything like this. My life was full of one precocious toddler and his everyday antics. It wasn't exactly designer dresses and Louboutin high heels.

But, once I was outside, those years of cotillion kicked back in. It was a bit like riding a bike. I stood straighter, let one foot move in front of the other, and pushed my shoulders back. I'd gone with a floor-length honey-yellow silk dress that fell off my narrow shoulders. My hair was swept up off my face, and my makeup was glamorous with pretty pink lipstick.

I felt like a million bucks, and when David caught a glimpse of me standing in front of the limo, it made all those hours at the spa worth it. His eyes gleamed with delight. His jaw dropped open on sight. And his body shifted in response, as if his world had tilted.

And mine had, too. Because David was wearing a perfectly cut black tuxedo that fit him like a dream.

"Wow," he said when he finally reached me.

"Wow yourself." I ran my hand down the front of his lapel. "Love the tux."

"And that dress," he breathed. "You look stunning."

"Thank you. After all that time at the spa, I should look decent."

"You always look better than decent." He placed a quick kiss on my lips. "But, tonight, you're glowing."

I smiled broadly up at him, and then he held the door open for me to get back into the limo. David followed close behind.

"You did a great job," he said to Katherine, gesturing to me.

"I am skilled, but I had a great canvas."

I laughed. "I was your project for the day?"

"Of course. These people expect something, and I wanted to give it to them."

"I don't think anyone expects anything from me."

Katherine arched an eyebrow. "Hardly." She caught David's eye. "Haven't you told her what it's really like? Especially for someone new?"

"It'll be fine," David said, taking my hand.

"Well, yes, I made sure of that." Katherine smiled brilliantly at me. "Don't worry; David's probably right. I'll be with you."

I didn't know what that meant. I'd seen plenty of these sorts of things on TV before. I'd been to so many events back home. It couldn't be that different.

Our driver pulled up in front of the MET a few minutes later and swiftly walked around to open the door. David went first and offered me his hand. I securely placed it in his to make sure I didn't make an idiot of myself. Then, I stepped out onto the sidewalk.

The MET was gorgeous—all white with dozens of stairs and long red banners hanging down between the columns. I was surprised to see a host of photographers congregated together and an array of tourists who had gathered to stare at us as we exited our vehicles.

"What is this for again?" I whispered to David.

"A charity, I'm sure."

I opened my mouth to ask which charity when Katherine stepped out of the limousine, and suddenly, I could hardly hear myself think. The photographers rushed forward toward the limo, cameras flashing, microphones raised, questions being asked. Katherine smiled coyly at them and then drifted forward toward the stairs. She waved at a handful of people and stopped for a photograph here and there, but otherwise, we just followed in her impressive wake.

"What did you say Katherine does?" I murmured.

"She's a socialite. She has her own perfume and helps with charities and sits in the front row during Fashion Week. It pains me to say it, but she's kind of an *it* girl."

And she was. That was clear, as it seemed every person nearby knew who she was. She waved at another couple and chatted briefly with a friend. She was her own orbit.

"I feel out of the loop," I admitted.

"It's a New York thing. It's not like she's in movies or TV or anything. This circle runs tight, and a lot of people don't know who anyone here is unless they either do something horrible or something extraordinary."

the WRIGHT ONE

David hadn't been wrong when he told me that he'd show me his world. And it was a whole new world. I might as well have been flying on a magic carpet.

It didn't matter that I had a trust fund the size of the state of Texas. Old money New York was a beast in itself.

But, beyond my own confusion over Katherine's big entrance, my own eyes were wide with excitement. This was kind of like walking through a dream. I kept expecting to wake up and find myself back in Lubbock, taking care of a toddler and working at the bakery. The glitz and glamour was fun for a night. Even though it wasn't my life, I could enjoy the extravagance of it all. Remember what it was like to have no cares in the world.

We finally made it up the stairs, through the MET, and into the European Sculpture Court. Designed to look like a French garden, seventeenth-century sculptures dotted the landscape and lined the walls. High-top tables were clustered into trios at various integrals, a bar was set up on either side of the room, and waiters were floating around with hors d'oeuvres and wine. It was stunning. While I'd been to the museum before, it had been some time, and I definitely had not adequately appreciated the artwork.

Katherine looped her arm into mine just as a waiter appeared before us. We each snagged a glass of champagne and then strolled deeper into the crowd swarming the exhibit. David followed at my side.

"What do you think?" he asked with a smile.

"It's amazing."

He nodded and glanced around, as if he were just remembering why all of this was so incredible. He'd been so cynical about his life, but it couldn't have all been bad.

We'd only made it a few feet into the room when a man stepped right into our line of vision. He had cunning eyes and a mocking smile. His tuxedo accentuated his broad shoulders and built frame. He was handsome and clearly knew it.

"Hello, Katherine," he said, taking her hand and placing a kiss on it. "My darling."

Katherine's smile was equally contemptuous, as if she were playing charades. "Camden."

Ah, the elusive Camden.

He clutched her hand in his and drew her closer. "Have you missed me terribly? It must have been such a tragedy to be without me this week."

"Terribly," she said as crisp as the Evil Queen's apple and just as poisonous.

"And what have we here?" He slid his gaze to David but never released Katherine. He moved his hand to her waist and held her—not...warmly, but more like he was keeping her in her rightful place. "Why...David Van Pelt. What a surprise."

"Camden," David said with a head nod. "This is my girlfriend, Sutton Wright. Sutton, Camden Percy."

"Nice to meet you," I said, offering him my hand.

Camden looked me up and down in the way that a viper might assess a mouse. Then, he forcefully shook my hand once.

He eyed Katherine. "I assume this is your doing."

"Be nice," Katherine warned.

"I'm always nice." The lie cut like glass.

I tipped back my champagne to ignore the awkwardness. David had been exaggerating about Katherine but not about Camden. He was worse than

David had made him seem. Every word was carefully chosen. Every syllable a mockery. It was stifling to be in his presence.

"You're a scoundrel," Katherine told him.

"I can't help it when you bring rabble into our midst and dress it up to look like class," he spat back.

I nearly choked on my champagne. "Rabble?"

"Nouveau riche," he clarified. "Don't take it personally. All new money has a look."

And the way he'd said it, it was clear he didn't think it was a *good* look.

"Enough," David said, low and menacing.

"It's fine," I assured him. "I don't have to justify myself or how much money my family has to anyone. Let alone him."

"I didn't ask for a justification," Camden said, squeezing Katherine's side. "I just pointed out that Oscar de la Renta doesn't hide that you don't belong here."

My cheeks bloomed pink with humiliation. The words hit me harder than they should have. Not because I wanted to *belong* in this strange world. But because he was pointing out the fact when I'd finally gotten comfortable in this skin Katherine had pasted over my own. I was here for fun, and now, I felt unwelcome.

"I said, that's enough," David said.

"What? If I hurt her feelings, will this one kill herself, too?" Camden asked with a sneer.

I gasped at the words.

But David saw red.

One minute, he was at my side; the next minute, he was flying across the space and ramming his fist into Camden Percy's face.

Thirteen

David

"David, no!" Sutton cried. She grabbed on to my sleeve to pull me away from Camden. Katherine gasped and stepped out of the way of the fight.

I was still up in Camden's face. He looked like he was ready to take a swing back at me. I hadn't broken his nose, but I'd fucking wanted to. That bastard, bringing that shit up to me in public, all casual as if it didn't still haunt me that Holli was dead. He was a dick. I had known that, going into this. I'd figured he'd say some shit about Sutton having the wrong kind of money, but I hadn't expected him to bring up ancient history.

I could feel eyes upon us from all directions. I knew I should step back, but man, I wanted to lay him out. How could Katherine marry him when he was such an atrocious human being?

"David!" Sutton yelled at me again.

My eyes flitted to her. She looked so frantic, so desperate. And that was the instant I knew that I'd stepped over the line. Fuck, I hated this guy.

I instantly backed away. "You're not worth it," I finally said.

"I was just speaking the truth," Camden spat.

"Your truth is laced with arsenic."

Camden shrugged and stuffed his hands into his pockets. His jawline was already swelling from where I'd hit him. My hand was throbbing, not that I'd ever let him see it.

Sutton stepped between us and glared at Camden, as if he weren't a Percy who owned more hotels than the Hiltons. "You're right; I don't belong here. But, if that means, I don't belong near you either, then I'd say that's a win."

Then, she held on to my arm and promptly marched us to the other side of the room. It wasn't until we were standing next to another naked sculpture that I realized her hands were shaking.

"Well, he's a royal jackass," Sutton grumbled.

"Understatement." I shook my hand out. One of the knuckles had split, and I hadn't even hit him as hard as I should have.

"You shouldn't have let him bait you like that."

"I didn't let him bait me," I told her. "I'd expected most of that conversation. I hadn't expected him to bring up Holli. My anger got the best of me."

"I understand that," she said on a sigh. "What he said was horrible."

"Yes, especially because what he said was untrue. No one was mean to Holli. She didn't kill herself because she was bullied. She did it because she was depressed, and this world fucking ruined her."

"I'm sorry," she said. She tilted her head as she assessed me. "Did you love her?"

"Holli?" I asked in surprise. "No. We weren't together like that. She was just my best friend. A lot of people thought we were together, but we weren't. I cared for her but not like that."

"I was trying to understand the situation. I mean, I know what it's like to live with the ghost of a dead loved one."

Her eyes were so sad. So sincere. It broke me to see that pain radiating out of her like that. To be so far away from the source on a night that was supposed to be pure magic and still ache from the inside out. I didn't want that for her. I didn't want any of this for her. She didn't need to see me in a fistfight or deal with my sister's horrible fiancé. She deserved way more than that.

"You know what?" I asked, straightening. "Fuck it. Let's just leave."

"Wait...what?"

"You've seen this part of my life. You've seen how awful it is, too." I took her hand in mine. "But this trip is also about us. And this isn't us. So, let's leave and find something better to do. We don't have to deal with this bullshit anymore. This is partly why I left anyway."

"Are you sure? What about Katherine?" Sutton asked.

"This is still her world. She'll survive."

Sutton laughed at my own enthusiasm, and I ducked down to plant a kiss on her lips.

"You'll go with me?"

"Of course," she murmured.

I took her hand in mine and then tugged her back toward the entrance. We almost made it out the door when Katherine appeared out of nowhere.

"What are you doing?" she asked.

"We're heading out," I told her. "Not quite my scene anymore."

"You're leaving?" she asked, aghast. "Where are you going?"

"Anywhere. Out."

"Come with us," Sutton told her. "You don't have to be here with them either."

Katherine eyed Sutton skeptically. "People will talk if I just disappear."

"Let them talk," I told her.

A sly smile appeared on her face. "All right. I know just the place, but let's slip out the side so as to draw less attention."

I grinned down at my sister in amazement. I never in a million years would have thought that she'd actually ditch this party. Not when this was practically her job. But the suggestion seemed to light her up, and within a few minutes, we were out a side exit and piling into a cab.

It was a short ride before we were dropped off outside of a Percy hotel. I couldn't help it; I laughed.

"What?" Sutton asked, glancing at the name. "Wait...is Camden a Percy, *Percy*?"

"He is," Katherine said.

"Oh...whoa."

"Yeah. But we're not going into the hotel. Just the roof."

"Ah, it feels like high school," I told Katherine.

She flicked her wrist as the bellboy opened the door for us. "Just because you disappeared from the city didn't stop any of us from living on rooftops."

We took the elevator up to the rooftop access and to what I assumed was Katherine's latest favorite rooftop bar. In front of a black door was a nondescript black sign that read *Bar 360*. Nothing else suggested what we were about to walk into, but I could take a guess.

Katherine pushed through the black door and smiled at the bouncer on the other side. We followed in her wake to find a three-hundred-sixty-degree panoramic view of the city skyline from the top of the Percy hotel. High-end clientele danced to the club music blasting through speakers. A bar wrapped around the inside of the roof. A glass-bottom infinity pool extended off the edge of the building. And, suddenly, it felt like déjà vu, living this life with Holli before her death and then desperately searching for the same high by hanging out with Court when she was gone.

"Are you okay?" Sutton called over the music.

"It's just weird, being back."

"I can imagine. This so isn't Lubbock."

I laughed and put my hand on the small of her back to guide her through the crowd to a reserved booth. Katherine pecked a kiss on the bouncer's cheek, who'd cleared the table for us.

"I think we're a bit overdressed," Sutton said, slinking into the booth.

"You can never be overdressed. Only underdressed," Katherine assured us.

"What she means is that she'll come back next week, and everyone will be wearing black tie because she showed up in formalwear," I told Sutton.

Katherine raised a shoulder. "As if I can help it."

A waitress in scantily clad lingerie appeared then with bottle service for the table. She poured drinks for us just as another familiar face appeared at our table.

"Penn!" Katherine cheered. "And, now, my night is a success." She batted her lashes at him and leaned in to kiss his cheeks.

I shook his hand. "Good to see you, man."

"Same," Penn said with a casual smile. His eyes flitted to Sutton, and he arched an eyebrow. "And you're Sutton, right?"

"Yes."

They shook hands.

"Sorry about the last time we met," Penn said, laying the charm on thick. "I didn't know that mentioning that David was a Van Pelt would cause such a stir."

"It's okay," Sutton said. "It all worked out in the end."

"What does it even matter if he's a Van Pelt?" Katherine asked. "He wasn't the one who stole your family's money."

"Katherine," I snapped.

Penn rested a hand on her shoulder. "Easy to lay blame at other's feet."

"I had a warped view of what y'all were like," Sutton said over the glass of champagne. "I thought you were all monsters. But I just didn't know you. I can see that's not true."

Katherine shot her a wicked grin. "Oh, darling, that is the most accurate thing you've said all weekend."

Penn scooted Katherine over and sank into the booth. "Not all of us are monsters, Ren."

She toyed with his tie and gave it a hard tug. "I do hope you're not talking about yourself. If history serves…"

"Let's leave history where it belongs," Penn said. He pulled his tie out of her grasp and draped an arm across the back of the booth. "Either way, I'm glad you're both here. It's nice to get Katherine out of her society events now and again."

Katherine tutted. "It's nice to get you in the Upper East Side at all."

Penn shrugged, unconcerned, and sent Sutton a charismatic smile. "Don't listen to a word she says. Care to dance?"

Sutton glanced at me once, and I nodded. "Uh…sure."

I let her out of the booth, and then Penn dragged her out into the mix. My eyes followed their movements, but it was strange then to be alone with my sister. I could feel her watching me.

"She's a little ray of sunshine," Katherine said.

"Isn't she?"

"She suits you. Maybe because you each lost someone important. It changed you. Shaped you. I don't think I really noticed until tonight."

"Well, you never were that observant."

She laughed and downed a shot of tequila.

"You're doing well around her."

"I don't know what you mean," Katherine said, her eyes twinkling. "And, anyway, *you're* the one who punched my fiancé."

"He had it coming."

"Assuredly."

"Do you really plan to marry him?"

Katherine shrugged. "Changes based on the day of the week."

I heard the sadness leak into my sister's voice, and I caught her eye. For a moment, I could see the facade she portrayed drop off of her. She was drowning. Camden was holding her under. Our parents only made it worse. She needed someone. She needed a safety net.

I reached across the table and took her hand. I was surprised she let me hold it. "I'm here now. You'll never be alone again, okay?"

She nodded and glanced back to where Penn and Sutton were dancing. "I'll be fine. I always am."

We both knew it was a lie.

"Come on. Let's cut in." I tugged her out of the booth. "Pretend it's like old times, and forget your worries for a night, Ren."

I could barely hear her over the music, but it drifted up to me.

"Thank you."

I'd never known how much I wanted to have my sister back until that moment. And I was only standing here in this moment because of Sutton Wright. She was turning my world upside down, and I was pretty sure she didn't even know it.

Fourteen

Sutton

"I really am sorry about what happened when I was in Lubbock," Penn said over the music.

"Honestly, it was for the better. Bad timing, but it got it all out there."

"I felt so bad about it, so I got him wasted."

I laughed unabashedly. There was something about Penn. He gave off diverging vibes. I could tell that he was a good guy, but then sometimes, I'd see his eyes slide to mine or a smile touch his lips, and I'd take it all back. I'd met guys like him in college. The ones who could charm your pants off with a glance. He was a wild card.

"It's really fine." I put my hands over my head and circled my hips to the beat. "Are you and Katherine…"

He raised his eyebrows. "Together?"

"Yeah. You seem compatible. Like…really easy around each other."

"We've been friends since we were children," he said and left it at that.

"Ah, like David and Holli."

Penn frowned. "Oh, yeah, that was a tragedy."

"It sounds like it."

I dragged him a little deeper into the crowd. I could feel people watching him. He was that attractive. When Annie had first seen him, I'd thought she was going to faint.

"Well, are you dating anyone?"

"You interested?" he joked with a wink.

"My best friend thought you were hot," I offered.

He laughed. "Currently unattached."

"She'll be glad to know that. Are you coming back to Lubbock for Jensen's wedding next weekend?"

"I'll be there. Are you going to play matchmaker?"

"Oh God, no," I told him on a chuckle. "You couldn't handle her."

That devious smile returned. "Try me."

For a split second, I could see that maybe even Annie would be out of her league with a guy like this.

David appeared then at my shoulder. "Mind if I cut in?"

I snapped my attention away from Penn and up into David's smiling face, thankful in that moment that I'd snagged the one nice guy from the Upper East Side. "Please do."

Katherine's arm slithered around Penn's waist and up the front of his suit. "Hello, lover."

David drew me into him until our hips touched as we swayed to the music.

I wrapped my arms around his neck. "I missed you."

"Didn't fall prey to Penn in the meantime?"

I shook my head. "Was thinking of how lucky I was that I got you actually."

"That is not the normal reaction to Penn Kensington."

"Well, I see that your sister is enamored with him."

"Always has been, but it's one-sided."

But, when David spun me around and pressed himself up against my ass, I let all thoughts about Penn and Katherine flutter out of my mind. His hands were on my body. His lips against the shell of my ear. Our hips moving in a rhythm I was well aware of.

We refilled my champagne glass endlessly while we danced to the pulsing of the music and soaked in the aura that encompassed New York City. I knew that I was going from tipsy to drunk to wasted when my movements became slow, and I felt like I was about to fall over at any minute, but I was having the time of my life. Penn and Katherine had disappeared deeper into the crowd. David and I had to press firmly against each other, as there was hardly any room to move.

I was hot, my heart was racing, and suddenly, I was horny as fuck.

Champagne seemed to be an aphrodisiac. Or maybe it was from being so uninhibited here with David. No responsibilities. No expectations. No rules. Just me and him.

And I really fucking liked it. I knew I'd have to go home tomorrow and settle back into the life I'd created for myself in Lubbock. But I wanted to live this night to its fullest.

My hands snaked to the back of David's neck, and I pulled his lips down to mine. Our tongues moved against one another, touching and teasing. I wanted all of him in that moment. My core was pulsing to the tempo. My fingers skimmed the front of his pants. He groaned into my mouth.

"Maybe we should head back to the hotel," he urged.

"Or maybe something closer," I reasoned.

"What do you have in mind?"

I took his hand, and he followed me out of the crowd. My brain told me that I should have more care, but I threw caution to the wind. For the first time in months and months, I actually felt exhilarated...even rebellious.

I located the one empty restroom that I'd seen when we first entered the club. David looked like he was going to protest, but I stumbled inside, and he hastily followed me, locking the door behind us.

"Sutton," he said as if he couldn't believe we were here right now. But, at the same time, he wasn't stopping.

I was just fucking glad that it was an individual restroom.

I reached for his waistband, unzipped his pants, and pushed them off his hips. His eyes were wide as I thrust my hand into his boxers and grasped his cock.

"We should probably—"

I cut off whatever he was about to say by sticking my tongue down his throat.

"Fuck," he murmured as I stroked him up and down.

I pushed him back against the door, rearranged my dress, and then sank to my knees right there on the restroom floor. I tugged his boxers lower, causing his cock to jut out toward me. I glanced up at him once, waiting to see if there was an ounce of protest. But none came.

Then, I licked him from the bottom of his shaft all the way up to the head. When I dragged the flat of my tongue across the tip, he shuddered at my touch. Pre-cum glistened in the slit, and I lapped the salty taste into my mouth.

His hand fisted into my hair. "Oh fuck."

I wrapped my mouth around the head, and then he slowly guided me all the way down. I took a breath as I moved back out. Then, I took him in fully again. My throat swallowed back the urge to gag, but I wasn't letting a bit of him go.

With my lips wrapped around him, I started to move back and forth. Slow at first and then a little faster as I worked up a momentum. I was still pretty drunk, so having him steady me was actually better. I worked him up until his shaft was practically throbbing with the need to orgasm.

"Sutton," he said, tapping my head, "I want to finish in you."

But I didn't dare move. I wanted this. I wanted him to finish in my mouth. When he realized that I wasn't about to get up to let him fuck me, both his hands moved to my head. He seemed unable to hold back control any longer. He held my head in place and then properly fucked into the back of my throat. It only took a few measured thrusts before I felt hot cum shooting into my mouth and down my throat.

He groaned as he finished, emptying himself entirely. I waited until he was finished and then swallowed, slowly dragging my mouth back. My jaw ached a little, but his eyes gleamed with heady desire and satisfaction.

I stood back up and carefully wiped my mouth just as someone banged on the door. David seemed to wake up at the reminder of where we were and what we'd just done.

He righted his clothing and then came after me. "My turn?"

"I don't think we have time."

"How close are you?" he demanded.

Then, his hand was under my dress. I wasn't wearing underwear, and his fingers stroked into my wetness. He firmly held me in place and started to circle my clit. The feverish banging from the patrons waiting for an empty restroom only hurried our passion.

"God, I want to fuck you right now," David said against my ear. "To feel you clenching around my cock as I thrust into you. To draw out that orgasm so completely that you'd be seeing stars for days."

His words opened something inside me; abruptly, my orgasm rocked through me, and I went straight over the edge.

I was still panting as I quickly straightened out my dress. A line had formed when we opened the restroom door and sheepishly left. One dude gave David a high five. I laughed. I couldn't even be bothered to be embarrassed. Maybe with less alcohol in a different place on a different night. But not tonight.

"I'm so glad we did this," David told me.

I arched an eyebrow. "Almost had sex in the restroom?"

"Came to New York. I feel reinvigorated. I feel like this was what our relationship needed. Like we're on the same page again."

"It really opened my eyes. I was so blinded by the Van Pelt name and feeling betrayed that I couldn't see past that. I'm just happy you opened yourself up to me. I know your life now as well as you know mine."

"You're exactly what I never knew I always wanted."

Then, he kissed me, and the world felt so right.

Fifteen

David

I woke up before Sutton the next morning. She was completely naked and sprawled out across the king-size bed. Her hair fanned out across a pillow, her lips slightly parted, and her breathing slow and steady. She was perfection in the early morning light.

We'd come back to the hotel and spent several hours in bed and on the balcony and in the Jacuzzi. We'd made full use of the hotel amenities, to say the least.

I was surprised to find that I wasn't ready to go back to Lubbock. I wanted to stay in New York in our little bubble. I knew it wasn't realistic. Sutton needed to get back to Jason, of course. And I desperately needed to return to Wright Construction. But it was nice for the time to be here like this.

My hand stroked gently down Sutton's exposed back, feeling every curve on her lithe body. I knew them intimately. I'd explored every one with my tongue last night. I was contemplating starting all over again when her eyelids fluttered.

"Mmm," she mumbled. "That feels good."

"Good morning." I placed a kiss on her cheek, and her eyes finally opened warily to catch the sun.

"It's early."

"It's almost eleven."

"Oh God," she groaned, rolling over and taking the sheets with her. "I don't remember the last time I slept until eleven."

"We did pull an all-nighter."

"I don't remember the last time I had one of those either."

I leaned forward over her, pulling her into a kiss. "We could work on that."

"Ugh, I need to brush my teeth," she said, pushing me backward.

I laughed. "No early morning sex without brushing your teeth?"

"Hey, dental hygiene is important."

"How about I don't kiss your mouth?" I suggested. Then, I slid down her body and kissed down her chest, over her stomach, and lower.

She squirmed but didn't protest.

Just as I was almost between her thighs, a loud knock sounded from the living area.

I groaned in frustration and looked up at Sutton. "We could ignore it."

"That seems wise," she said with a giggle.

Then, the knocking sounded again and louder.

"Ugh!" I grumbled. "I'll be quick. It's probably just the maid service."

I jumped out of bed and hastily threw on a pair of shorts and a T-shirt before heading toward the front door.

"I'm coming. I'm coming," I said as someone knocked again.

Without even glancing into the peephole, I unbolted the door and jerked it open. I was prepared for a monologue about proper service at this kind of hotel. Especially in a penthouse suite. I was prepared for anything…except my mother.

"Hello, darling," Celeste Van Pelt said with a pert smile.

My eyes drifted over my mother's face, which had aged some in the last eight years. Though not as much as it should have, thanks to plastic surgery. She wore her classic Chanel suit, complete with pantyhose and her favorite pair of Manolo Blahnik heels. She looked exactly as I remembered her…and not at all.

"What are you doing here?" I asked, struck dumb.

"That would be because of me," Katherine said.

I finally realized that she was standing next to our mother and had been all along. She was out of her floor-length party dress and in an outfit more fit to be seen out on a Sunday morning. More fit to be seen with our mother.

"I thought I told you that I didn't want to talk about our parents or anything to do with the fallout and that I had absolutely no interest in seeing them either." My eyes flicked to my mother's when I said it. She didn't even blink at the tone.

"Yeah, well," Katherine said with a shrug, "you didn't actually expect me to keep that promise, did you?"

"Why don't you invite us in?" Celeste suggested.

"This should be great."

But manners kicked in, and I opened the door wide for them to come in.

I was second-guessing being nice to Katherine for the last couple of days. She'd been on her best behavior, and I remembered what it was like to have family again. But this underhanded bullshit was quintessential Katherine. It didn't sit well with me. Worse yet, she had known that it wouldn't and had done it anyway.

I slammed the door shut behind them and then hurried to make sure there wasn't any incriminating evidence of my time with Sutton last night and to warn her about what kind of shitshow she was about to walk into. But, before I could do either, a bleary-eyed Sutton appeared then in nothing but my oversize T-shirt.

She rubbed her eyes. "Who was at the door?" she asked. Then, she seemed to take in the surroundings and the fact that Katherine was here...with someone else. Her cheeks heated. "Uh...sorry. I'll just, uh...be right back."

Then, she darted back into the bedroom as fast as she could.

I hit my forehead in frustration and glared at my mother and Katherine. "Thanks for that."

Katherine shrugged. "We'll wait."

I ground my teeth and then hurried after Sutton. She was standing in the bathroom, running a brush through her hair to try to tame the knots that had formed from last night.

"Hey, sorry about that," I told her.

"It's okay. Just one of the more humiliating things that has ever happened to me."

"I didn't know Katherine was going to show up, and I didn't think she'd bring my mom at all. I told her not to talk to me about it, especially in front of you."

"Yeah…I gathered that she hadn't listened to you. I recognized your mom from the news," she admitted sheepishly. "And I'd walked out there without pants on. That's going to just go down in the hall of fame as one of the most embarrassing moments of my life. I'll have you know that this will play prominently in my nightmares for basically ever."

I couldn't help but laugh at how intense she was at the moment. But her glare dropped it off my face.

I moved in and planted a kiss on her cheek. "I'll still love you either way."

Sutton nearly dropped the brush in her hand. Her eyes widened, and a smile broke out on her face. "What did you just say?"

Then, I realized that I'd said that thing I'd been thinking for so long. I hadn't even processed that it had just come out of my mouth. It had just felt so natural.

"I love you," I told her. "I know I probably shouldn't just blurt it out like this. And that we're still working on our relationship. And that there's so much more we need to figure out together."

"David."

"Yeah?"

"Shut up," she said. Then, she threw her arms around my neck and kissed me.

I held her close to me. "It's not too soon?"

"No," she breathed against my lips. "I feel like I should be more uncertain about this. But I've been so uncertain for so long, so afraid to feel like this again.

And, now...I'm not afraid anymore." She paused, as if she were testing the words out in her mind, before saying, "I love you, too."

I kissed her again. Hearing those words from her was like a balm. I suddenly felt as if I could take on the world. It didn't matter that, in ten seconds, I'd have to face my mother for the first time in nearly a decade. I was on top of the world. And, with Sutton at my side, I could surely endure this, too.

"Okay, okay. Go find out what your mom wants," Sutton said with a grin. "I'll be in once I manage to look presentable."

Our lips met once more, and then I reluctantly pulled away. I really didn't want to leave this room, only to face my mother again. But it seemed there was no other choice.

I didn't bother dressing up for my mother. She'd essentially disowned me as a Van Pelt when I had tried to do everything right. I didn't need to impress her now. I strode back into the sitting area and found Katherine on the phone, calling downstairs for tea.

"I guess you've made yourself at home," I drawled.

"Everything is better handled with tea," Celeste said.

"And here I thought, you'd prefer a Bloody Mary."

"Not for this chat."

Chat. As if we were going to talk about her next charity function instead of how I hadn't seen her in so long. Or you know, the millions of dollars in fraud she'd gotten away with stealing while my father took all the blame. I knew she wasn't innocent. She knew that I knew she wasn't innocent. Yet here we stood, staring back at each other, as if we were perfect strangers.

"Couldn't we have had this chat somewhere else? With some warning?"

"You and I both know that you never would have met me out in public. I haven't seen my son in eight years, and I wasn't going to let you slip out of the city without seeing you now."

"Oh, so I'm your son now."

My mother's eyes were sad when they looked at mine, but otherwise, her face showed nothing. "Why don't we sit before we throw around accusations?"

I didn't bother sitting. I strode around the room and waited for the tea to show up and for Sutton to come out here. I didn't particularly want to have this conversation in front of her, but I felt stronger with her here.

Whatever Katherine had said must have gotten the room service to move their ass because it was only a few minutes before it was carted in. Then, Sutton appeared, looking like a spring flower, and we all took our seats. Katherine poured tea. Awkwardness pervaded everything.

"You must be Sutton," Celeste said. "I've heard a great deal about you from my daughter."

Sutton's eyes flicked to Katherine's and back. "I am. And you must be Celeste Van Pelt."

"Yes. I'm sure you've heard your fair share about me as well."

"I have, but I'm just here for David."

"I'm glad that my son has someone to be there for him." She took a sip of her tea and then looked at me again. "I came here today because I missed you."

I was so taken aback that I stared blankly for a moment before saying, "I find that shocking."

"I know that I wasn't the best mother, but I did try to do right by you."

"If that's what you'd like to call it."

"David," Katherine snapped, "she's trying."

"Is she?"

Celeste met my gaze. "We…I shouldn't have said the things that I said to you all those years ago. You came to me with the truth, and I took it out on you. It was wrong of me, for both of us, to do that when they were our mistakes," she said quietly. "But you are my son whether I birthed you or not. I want that relationship back. I want you back."

"You could have reached out to me at any point. You knew what I'd changed my name to. You knew where my biological parents were. You even probably knew how horrible they were."

She nodded. "I needed you to see it for yourself."

"But you never came to get me. You never came to see me."

"I did," she admitted. "Once. I flew out to San Francisco to ask you to come home, but when I got there, I saw that you were so happy with your new family. I believed I'd made a mistake, and by interfering, I'd only drive you away further."

Sutton reached across the couch and took my hand in hers. She gently squeezed it, letting me know she was here, that she understood the enormity of what was happening.

I found it impossible to believe that my mother had done such a thing. So out of character for her. But, when I looked at the beautiful woman who had raised me, I realized that maybe I hadn't given her enough credit. The last couple of years had been hard on her. I tried to imagine what it might be like for Sutton if she lost Jason. Utterly devastating. I couldn't imagine my own mother that distraught, but...it was possible.

Seeing her here, now, not quite apologizing, but giving as much of an apology as Celeste Van Pelt ever would, it made me stop and reconsider everything.

"I never turned you in," I told her. "I know that I said I would, but...I never did."

"I wouldn't have blamed you if you had. But we dug our own grave. It was only fitting that we had to lie in it."

"Do you really want to have a relationship with me again?" Somehow, the words were still stuck in my throat.

"More than anything," my mother said.

I nodded, not finding the words. Then, to my surprise, my mother stood and hugged me. Not a careful, uncertain thing, but a real hug.

And, when she pulled away, I saw Sutton's eyes were misted with tears. That Katherine was trying to hide her own relief that her plan had worked. I stood in awe that I was even considering starting a new relationship with my mother. That I actually wanted this despite everything that had happened. Maybe it wouldn't be the same, but in the end...that was probably for the better.

Sixteen

Sutton

Yes, I cried for David.

And I cried later that night when I held Jason in my arms again. Skype just was not good enough. As much as I'd enjoyed my weekend in New York, there was nothing like holding my son. Absolutely nothing like being back in my house with him even if I could hear the ghosts again.

But I tried to push that pain away. What really mattered was that David had gone eight long years without a mother, and now, they were going to work toward a relationship again. It almost felt too good to be true. Like I'd expected Celeste Van Pelt to somehow live up to her villainous name. For her to cackle like Cruella de Vil and traipse off into the shadows in a mink coat. Except she had been genuine, and that one trip to New York City had spun it all into motion.

Even though Jason had his own bed, I let him crawl into bed with me. I brushed his hair back, which looked so like his daddy's, and watched him fall to sleep, knowing I was so lucky. So very lucky. I might not have his father anymore, but there was a big piece of him right here with me.

Having Jason close again lulled me to sleep, and I woke early the next morning, feeling remarkably rested for someone with a toddler.

It was probably the afterglow of New York. Of David telling me he loved me.

I'd thought for so long that it would be impossible to love again.

That Maverick's death had sapped the love right out of me.

Seeing other people's happiness had felt like a stab to the chest. Even though I'd wanted my family to be happy, it had still hurt, knowing that I'd been the happiest of them all and it had been callously stolen from me. Now, I had new happiness…something entirely new. And it made me both ecstatic and worried. Would this get torn away, too?

I hated second-guessing, but when something so horrible had happened, it was impossible *not* to.

I shook my head and went about getting Jason ready for the day. Jenny would be here soon. I needed to stop stressing and embrace this. That was what Maverick would have wanted. That was how we had always been together, and he wouldn't have wanted me to do anything else now.

I'd told David I loved him. I meant it.

And, now, I was ready to show that to the world.

the WRIGHT ONE

I picked up my phone and dialed David's number. It was early, but I knew he'd be up. Probably just coming out of the gym, working off the extra calories he'd consumed in New York this weekend. The thought brought a quick smile to my face.

"Good morning, beautiful," David said when he answered the phone.

"Morning," I said. "I wish I were waking up next to you. Though I had another man to keep me company."

"Oh, yeah? Do I need to beat someone up?"

"Depends. Can you measure up to someone who is about twenty-eight pounds?"

David clucked his tongue twice. "I don't know. He could probably take me."

"Probably. He does have a voracious appetite."

"And such a lucky guy, having such a great mom."

I beamed. It was impossible not to smile when someone called me a great mom. "So, I just remembered that my cousin and aunt are officially moving into town this afternoon. I know that Julian and Jordan will be there to help with moving and likely the rest of my family because that's just the kind of people we are. Do you have any interest in going?"

"I could be persuaded. How much heavy lifting will be involved?"

"Probably a lot for you and none for me."

"Seems fair." David paused on the line for a second. "What are you going to say to your family?"

"What do you mean?"

"Do they know that we're dating again? We kind of just jetted off for New York. I don't know if you've told them or if it's going to be awkward."

"Right," I said.

For some reason, it had completely slipped my mind that I hadn't told anyone about this. Everyone had been so busy with the wedding, and Jason's grandparents had taken him for the weekend. Of course, Morgan knew because David had gotten the time off on Friday. But...my nosy brothers didn't know.

"Still want to do this?"

"Yes," I said at once. "If I'm happy, they should be fine."

"Does that sound like them?"

"It'll be fine," I repeated. "I'll text you the address and meet you after work."

"Can't wait."

My stomach twisted at the thought of how this was going to go down with my family. They had my back. They loved me. I knew that they would do anything for me. But they were also overbearing, and I wasn't really looking forward to dealing with their judgment. As if they were all perfect.

Pfft!

I hurried home after work to grab Jason and let Jenny off the hook.

"Where are you off to?" she asked, gathering her things.

"My aunt moved into town today with Julian. I'm going over to help them move."

Jenny raised her eyebrows. "I didn't realize they were moving this soon."

"Yeah. I guess they rented a house in the meantime, so they could get started with her breast cancer treatments."

"How awful."

"I know. I think Jordan is staying in Vancouver until they can find a replacement for him in the Canadian branch of Wright, and then he's going to join them."

Jenny tucked a loose strand of hair behind her ear. "Need an extra set of hands?"

My eyebrows rose. "I thought you had test prep."

"Not until later tonight. I could…go with you."

"You want to see Julian?"

"Maybe…"

"Grab Jason's bag, and let's go," I said with a laugh.

Only a couple of minutes later, we secured Jason into the car seat, and we drove to the rental property. If the line of cars in front of the house was any indication, they probably didn't need our help moving, but we parked and entered anyway.

As I'd expected, the house was full of people. My family really knew how to roll out the red carpet. My brothers were busy with helping my cousins carry assorted furniture out of the moving van that had just shown up. Jenny gestured off to the side, as if to say she was going to find Julian, and then left.

Aunt Helene waved when we walked up to where she was seated in a lawn chair. "Hello, dear." She smiled at Jason. "And hello there, Jason."

Jason promptly hid behind my leg. He wasn't shy once you got to know him, but he was definitely in that clingy stage otherwise.

"It takes him a minute to warm up."

"That's fine. I'll be around for a long while, and I would love to get to see him more. He's adorable."

"Thank you. How are you feeling?"

"I'm fine," Helene said. "Just taking it one day at a time."

"Well, if there's anything I can do, please don't hesitate to ask."

"You all are so kind. I really do regret not coming down here sooner."

A dark cloud crossed over her face. I wondered if she was thinking about how my uncle Owen had hamstrung her for all those years. He'd left a foul taste in my mouth. It wasn't a good thing to bring up in front of Morgan either. She would go postal. With good reason.

I spoke with Helene for a few more minutes and let Jason gradually warm up to her. Once she pulled out children's books, I knew that she had him. By that time, my eyes were drawn to the front door. In walked David, still in his suit from work. I didn't know how he was going to lift boxes in that, but who was I to complain about a well-cut suit?

Morgan followed in behind him. Her eyes flitted between me and David, and then she winked at me. I laughed, made sure Jason was okay with Helene, and then approached them.

"Hey, Mor."

"Sutton," she said. "I see things are in better shape than when I last saw y'all."

"They are," I agreed.

"No more lying or hiding?" Morgan asked David.

He shook his head. "No more hiding. This is who I am."

"Good," Morgan said. "I get tired of always putting my siblings' relationships back together."

I swatted at her arm. "Hey now. Last I checked, I had to put you and Patrick back together."

"Speaking of," Morgan said, glancing around the room, "where is my man?"

"He's in the garage," Austin called as he hauled in a chair with Landon. "Carrying in boxes and leaving the hard stuff to us men."

Morgan rolled her eyes dramatically. "I'm sure that's exactly what's happening."

"He's actually carrying in all the boxes of books," Landon said. "There's probably a hundred of them, and they're all backbreakers."

"Hope there's a fucking library, is all I'm saying," Austin grumbled.

They set the chair down, and my brothers staggered over to us. Landon rubbed his back.

"Should you be doing that?" I asked.

Landon had injured his back in what we all thought was a career-ending move. He'd taken eighteen months off, and he was back at it again. It was kind of a miracle.

"Probably not. I have a clean bill of health, but I'm starting back full-time on the circuit in the fall. Can't afford any new injuries."

"Maybe leave the heavy stuff to the other idiots," Morgan said.

That was about the moment when Austin realized that David was standing there with us.

His brows furrowed, and his jaw clenched. "What the fuck are you doing here?"

David seemed unfazed. "I came to help."

"Your help isn't needed."

I put my hand out between Austin and David before Austin got it in his thick skull to punch David again. "It's okay. We're okay here."

"He *lied* to you. To all of us."

"Yeah," I agreed. "He did. But so did Julia, and you seemed to have forgiven her."

"That was different!"

"Maybe, but this is different, too. You don't know why he did what he did. We all jumped to conclusions instead of thinking about it reasonably."

"Maybe you're not thinking about it reasonably, Sut," Austin said in frustration. "I told him, if he ever hurt you, I'd kill him. Then, he totally fucked this up, and you're just going to let him back in your life. It's hardly been any time at all."

"First off, I can handle this myself. Second, you do not get to kill people. Nor do you need to threaten anyone. David and I are together, okay? You might think it's too soon, but that's just how it is."

"I want what's best for you," Austin argued. "You deserve the best. Not some trumped up Van Pelt masquerading as one of us."

"Austin, back off," Morgan said.

"Yeah, I think Sutton can handle this," Landon agreed.

David still hadn't said anything. He was standing there, taking the assault Austin was laying on him. I hated that he let Austin say whatever he wanted. He didn't deserve this.

"Why are you all on his side?" Austin asked in confusion. He looked between his siblings. "What do we really know about this guy? It's not been very long. Hardly enough time to even verify whatever spin he put on his story. This isn't the right move."

"Austin, I appreciate you looking out for me," I said calmly. "But fuck off."

"Sut—"

"No, you don't get to say these things about me or David. Now is not the time. I love you. And, if you love me, you'll accept that I'm happy. David makes me happy."

David moved forward then and extended his hand. "I never want to hurt her again. Truce?"

Austin looked at all of our earnest faces. He shook his head and then grabbed David's hand. "Don't fuck this up again."

"I have no intention of doing that."

I sighed with relief as the tension dissipated between them.

David went off with my brothers to help them bring more boxes inside. And I was left thinking about all the things Austin had just thrown in my face. He wasn't wrong exactly. It had been fast. David and I had rushed things a bit. But we'd deal with those things later and work it out together. I knew I wasn't going to fix trust issues overnight. I just hated that I was even thinking about this.

We'd had one blissful weekend, and now, we were back to reality. Reality sucked.

Seventeen

Sutton

"Sutton," Jenny whispered, dragging me away from the rest of my family later that day. She looked practically giddy.

"What's going on?"

"I know this is last minute, but do you think you could find a sitter for Jason tomorrow?"

"Tomorrow?" I asked. My eyebrows rose to the ceiling. "It's already evening. Who am I going to find on such short notice?"

"I don't know. I'm sorry. His grandparents?"

"What is this all about, Jen?"

Her eyes darted back to the living room and then to me again. "Julian asked me out."

"Oh my God!" I squealed, jumping up and down. "That's so exciting."

Jenny blushed. "It was unexpected, for sure. I thought, when he went back to Vancouver, that would be the end. And, now, it looks like it was only the beginning."

"Well, let me call Linda and see if she's free tomorrow. I'm sure she'd be happy to watch him while I'm at work."

"Thank you, thank you, thank you. If it doesn't work out, then, of course, I'll still be there, but I'd love to say yes to this."

I nodded understandably and then pulled out my phone. It only took one ring before Linda answered and a quick conversation before she emphatically agreed to watch Jason. She even said she'd come over to the house in the morning to be there when I left. I gave Jenny a thumbs-up, and she actually jumped up and down.

"I'm going to go tell him. Thanks, Sutton."

I waved her off, and David appeared then. "Everything all right?"

"Yeah. Julian asked Jenny out for tomorrow, so I'm having Linda look after Jason."

"That's new."

I laughed. "Uh, not really. They kind of started talking when he was visiting."

"I thought Annie and Jordan—"

"Yeah. Them, too."

David kissed the top of my head. "I wish I could come home with you."

"Maybe you could?" I suggested.

He laughed. "What about Jason?"

My eyes flitted to my son, who had snagged Austin's attention. He was now carrying Jason on his shoulders around the room.

"I should probably get him home. His bedtime is going to come sooner than I'd like."

"Next time," David assured me.

I leaned in for another kiss. "Maybe after Linda leaves tomorrow?"

"I'll come by for a bit. Maybe bring some pizza?"

"Sounds like a plan."

The next day, Linda came by for Jason, as planned. Work dragged while I counted down the minutes until I could leave. Then, I could see both Jason and David in the same place. I'd been putting that off. And I was pretty sure I was ready. Despite what Austin had said about us moving too fast.

By the time my shift ended, I was already throwing the apron on a hook and darting toward my Audi parked out back. I zipped across town and saw Linda's Toyota parked out front.

"Hey, Linda!" I said with a smile. "How did today go?"

"Mommy!" Jason cried, wrapping his arms around my legs.

"Hey, buddy." I picked him up and crushed him to me with a big bear hug. Then, I walked him over to the couch and sat down with him in my lap.

"Today was excellent. We went to the park and swimming at the pool. He's such an excellent swimmer already."

"Early lessons," I said. "They really paid off."

"We had a great day. You know, you could always get rid of that nanny, and I could do this full-time for you."

"Don't you need to help on the farm?"

"Well, yes, but Jason could help me with everything that I need. Maverick did the same thing at that age."

My heart panged at the name. It frequently echoed through my mind, but hearing it right now while holding Jason and thinking about another man…it was too hard. I tried to remind myself that it was okay in these moments to remember him. I didn't want to forget him. But talking about him, even to his mother, made it feel like I was trying to swallow peanut butter.

"Maybe, once Jenny gets into pharmacy school, we could revisit this conversation."

"Of course," Linda said. "You never told me how New York was. Did you miss Jason?"

"Terribly, but it was wonderful."

I kissed Jason on the forehead, and then he rushed into his room, likely to grab some more of his favorite books. He loved hanging out and flipping through every single book on his shelf.

"It was nice to have a weekend to myself. I'm sure you know, as a mom, we don't get a lot of time to ourselves."

"Well, you have a nanny and grandparents. It looks like you get a lot of time to yourself."

I clenched my jaw at those words. I was constantly with Jason. I didn't have Jenny for the weekends, and just because I was finally having a relationship didn't mean I was neglecting my time with Jason.

"One weekend off in two years seems justifiable."

"Two weekends," Linda reminded me.

"Well, the other was for a bachelorette party."

That didn't seem to matter to her.

"I think you're spending a lot of time away from Jason. I worry about him."

"You don't have to worry about him."

"I'm his grandma; of course I do. Especially since Maverick is gone."

I clenched my teeth. I didn't want to be having this conversation. David would be here in the next hour, and I was ready for Linda to leave. Thinking of Maverick made my heart hurt, and reminiscing with Linda was always a treasure, but I just couldn't do it right now. Not with the judgment and distaste. If she just wanted to talk to me about Maverick, I would always be there. But, if she wanted to make me feel bad, I was too tired.

"Are you bringing that boy around Jason?" Linda asked.

"No, I haven't been, but I'm about to start."

Linda clucked her tongue on her teeth. "As I suspected."

"What? What did you suspect? That I'd start dating someone else, and it would freak you out? I can't help how you feel, but I don't want you to try to control how I feel."

"I'm looking out for Jason!" Linda said, jumping to her feet. "Someone has to."

"Being upset like this isn't going to change my relationship with David."

"It's been a year, Sutton," Linda cried. "A year. I know it's normal for people to take off their black mourning clothes after that time, but you don't just forget him. And that's what you're doing. You're trying to forget Maverick. But I can't forget him. He's my son—my only son—and now, he's gone."

"I'm not forgetting him." I buried my face in my hands. "I can't forget him, okay? But I can be happy and move on. And I'm not saying David is perfect. He's not. He didn't tell me he was a Van Pelt. He held back his past from me. There's still a lot about him I don't know. But I do know that I love him."

Linda took a step back, as if I'd slapped her. "You *love* him?"

"Yeah," I whispered.

Linda shook her head in disbelief. Then, something seemed to dawn on her. "Van Pelt? Like that criminals who has been on the news?"

I realized my mistake too late. I'd been so busy with trying to argue my case that I didn't even realize what I'd said. Linda hadn't known that David was a Van Pelt. In fact, very few people did. But she did know about the Van Pelts. Most people did. Especially since it was on the news again.

"Uh…"

"You are letting a criminal into your life…into Jason's life?"

"No. He's not a criminal."

"His parents are criminals! They steal money. What do you really know about him? How do you know he's not getting close to you just to steal from you?"

"He's not…he'd never."

Linda shook her head in horror. "Jason isn't safe. You're not safe, Sutton. You don't even know this man, and suddenly, you've forgotten your husband, your son, your life. You're entrusting everything to this person you don't even know after only a couple of weeks?"

"That isn't—"

"Oh no," Linda cut me off. She straightened her spine. "I can't let Jason stay here."

"Excuse me?" I snapped.

"I'm going to have to call the authorities."

I raised my eyebrows. "You are going to do *what?*"

"You cannot be with this man. You don't even know what he could do to you, to your family. You're negligent with Jason. If you don't get your act together, then I'm going to have to do something drastic."

"What the hell are you talking about?" I asked, raising my voice as fear crept into my spine.

The way she was talking was insane. Totally crazy. And yet it was clear that she meant every word. That her own fear and grief and torment were pushing her over the edge.

"If you don't leave this man, then…I'll have to take you to court for Jason."

Silence.

Then, a ringing in my ears. A horrible ringing.

"No," I said. "Don't you *dare* threaten me with that. Jason is my son. I am his mother. I work a steady job. I have a trust fund. My family is well known, and we have more lawyers for our family than you've met in a lifetime. There is *no* way you could win that battle, which means you're just saying that to hurt me."

"I'll do it," Linda cried.

"It's futile. I'm a *Wright!*" I said it with such conviction and had never been happier to have my last name. "In this town, I'm royalty. There's no way you would win. Not a chance in hell. And, if you're going to come into my house and threaten me and my son, then you can get the hell out."

I pointed at the door. All the fire and anger shot through me at the empty accusations, and I was in mama-bear destruction mode at the thought of someone getting near Jason.

"Sutton," Linda tried to reason.

"I said, *get out*," I barked. "And don't come back until you've gotten some sense. I wanted you in his life. I wanted him to grow up with grandparents to love him since mine were gone. I wanted him to have a piece of Maverick. But I will no longer allow you near him. You threaten me, and we're done. No one—and I mean, *no one*—is going to take my son away from me."

Linda opened and closed her mouth. Then, she snatched her purse up and strode from the room. I locked the door behind her, and then I stumbled back into the living room and collapsed onto the couch.

Jason appeared then with worry on his little face. "Mommy?"

"Hey, buddy."

He stepped forward, put his hands on my cheeks, and brushed the tears away that had slipped out of my eyes. He leaned forward and kissed me on the lips. My heart ached, and he knew it. And he was trying to make me feel better, which only made me cry harder.

"Come here, you."

He jumped onto the couch and snuggled up against me. This was exactly where I wanted to be.

I hated what Linda had said. I hated what I'd had to say to her. I hated everything in that moment, except my son, who I would fight for with my last breath. I prayed that Linda wouldn't make me do just that.

Eighteen

David

It was raining, and I'd forgotten a damn umbrella again.

I darted out of Wright Construction and straight toward my shiny red Ferrari. By the time I made it into the car, I was soaked through. Just fucking awesome.

I hated the rain in Lubbock. It'd come out of nowhere in the middle of the afternoon like a beach thunderstorm, poured until all the streets flooded, and then stopped just as suddenly. Except today it hadn't freaking stopped, and my Ferrari really hated the flooding. I really hated the flooding. The entire city hated the flooding. And there was nothing we could do about any of it.

The drive to Sutton's was full of people who acted as if they'd never seen water fall out of the sky. That meant I was constantly weaving in and out of traffic while everyone else drove like morons. In New

York, I'd never had a car or even driven anywhere, and I'd *still* been a better driver than this shit.

Luckily, it was only a fifteen-minute drive, I picked up a pizza, and then I was parked outside of Sutton's house. I was excited about today. Letting me back into Jason's life was a big step for her. And I was ready for it. I adored her son. It'd been surprisingly difficult to be locked out of his life, considering I'd babysat him for the last year before Sutton and I even started dating.

I rushed across the flooded sidewalk, and my shoes squelched as they filled with water. I knocked on the door, shaking the water out of my hair, and hoping the pizza was okay as I waited for Sutton to answer.

But there was no reply.

I knocked again.

Still nothing.

Is no one home? She'd told me to come over after work when Linda was gone. *Is Linda still there? Did I need to come back?*

I pulled out my phone to text her right when the front door popped open. And there stood Sutton. Still in her work clothes with puffy, red eyes.

"Hey, what's wrong? Are you okay?"

She sniffled and shook her head.

"Okay. Let me come in and dry off, so I can hug you."

She opened the door wider, put her finger to her lips, and gestured to the living room. I stepped inside and saw what she was referring to. Jason was passed out on the couch.

The WRIGHT ONE

"I don't think he got a nap with Linda. He fell asleep right away when we were lying down," she whispered.

I nodded and deposited the pizza on the table in the entranceway. I was careful to be as quiet as possible as I emptied my shoes of water and hung my suit jacket on the coat rack. She gestured to the bedroom, and I followed her, leaving Jason to take his nap.

"So, what happened?"

Sutton sighed and sank onto the bed. "I accidentally told Linda who you were when she was on a rampage about me dating."

"Okay..."

"And she'd heard of your parents."

"Pretty much everyone has."

"Well, she kind of flipped her shit. She was already upset about me leaving two weekends in the last month. And I guess she's pissed that I have a nanny."

"You work full-time."

"I know," she whispered. "But I guess that's not good enough for her. I think she wants to watch him full-time, and she was upset that I hadn't asked her, but she never said anything. So, now, I'm left with her anger."

"Okay, that seems like it's all on her though."

"Yeah. It is. But...she accused me of not putting Jason's interests first. Then, she said you were dangerous."

"Dangerous?" This didn't sound good.

"A criminal. Or whatever."

"I am not a criminal," I said in disgust. "Why the hell would she say that about me? She doesn't even know me. We've never even met."

"Yeah. I know. I told her you weren't. But then she just freaked out. She threatened to take Jason away from me."

"She did *what*?"

I didn't think that she could have surprised me more if she'd punched me in the face. Linda must have been completely out of her mind. How could she threaten something that outrageous?

Sutton wiped at her tears again. "God, I was so strong when she was here, and now, I'm such a mess. She said she'd take me to court. When she said it, something in me combusted, and I told her I didn't want her in Jason's life if she was going to threaten me."

"Good. That's the nicest thing you could have said to her."

I reached out to try to comfort her, but she ripped away from me and stalked across the room.

"No, that's awful. I can't believe I told her I didn't want her in his life."

"Sutton, she threatened you and your son."

"I know, but we should have been able to figure this out. She just reacted, and we should have been calm and acted like adults and talked it over. I *want* her in Jason's life. She and Ray are the last parts of Maverick that Jason has."

"You did everything right here. You gave her every opportunity to be a part of his life. But you can't let her walk all over you."

Sutton paced the room. I could see the machinations of her mind going in a million different directions. "This never would have happened if I hadn't gone to New York."

"Are you hearing yourself?" I asked in dismay. "This is not because you took one weekend off. This has been brewing since the one-year anniversary. They're grieving."

"I'm grieving!" she shouted at me.

I held my hands up and took a step back. "I know. I understand that. But he was their son."

"He was my husband," she countered.

"I know," I said soothingly. "But I really don't know why you're even listening to a thing that she said."

"Because what if she's right?"

"Right about what? You're not a bad mom. You don't neglect your son. You're not dating a criminal. She's trying to get a rise out of you, and you're giving it to her."

"She's not just trying to get a rise out of me. She adamantly believes what she's saying. And maybe, if I stopped for a minute and considered it, I'd see where she was coming from."

"Why? Why do you have to see where she's coming from? You're happy. We're happy. Why won't you let yourself be happy?"

"Because he's gone!" she cried. "He's gone, and I'm here. And, sometimes, nothing about that makes sense."

"That's survivor's guilt talking. It's okay to feel that way, but that's not reality. We just had an amazing weekend. That's where you are right now, and Linda is manipulating you to feel bad about that."

"No one is manipulating me. I know exactly how I feel."

"And how do you feel, Sutton? Because, from where I'm standing, I feel like we're in the same damn place we started."

"I don't know. I don't know. This all just happened. And I don't know."

"You don't know," I said, monotone.

I shook my head in disbelief. I couldn't believe the words coming out of her mouth. After New York, after I'd laid everything out for her, told her things no one else knew, groveled…after everything, she still didn't know what we were doing here. She was still letting other people and fear dictate her own emotions. I knew this part of the grieving process, yet it felt insane that we were standing here, in this moment, when things had been utterly perfect only a few short days ago.

"What do you want me to say?"

"It doesn't matter what I want you to say," I told her. "Do you still want to be with me?"

"That's not it at all, David," she said. "Of course I want to be with you. I just think I should take other people's feelings about this into consideration."

"You want to take other people's feelings into consideration about how *you* should feel and who *you* should date? That makes no sense. What that sounds like is that you don't really want this. That you can't actually make up your mind one way or another, so you're using Linda and probably Austin to justify it."

"No, that's not it," she murmured.

"I want this. I told you about my parents and my biological parents. I confided in you about Holli because I thought you'd understand where I was coming from. I even had you meet my sister and then my mom. I've never put myself out there like this before. Not with anyone."

"I know; I know. This is about Jason."

"I think this is about you."

She ran a shaky hand back through her hair. "Maybe it is about me."

"I'm all in, Sut," I told her, "but, fuck, are you?"

She didn't answer me right away, and that seemed like answer enough. I clenched my jaw and nodded.

"Okay," I said. "Okay. Why don't you think on that and get back to me? I don't think I can grovel any more than I already have to get you to see where I'm at with you. This is what I want. I put it all on the line. If that's not what you want, then…I don't know what else I can do."

I turned and walked out of her bedroom. I heard a sob escape her, and it took everything in me not to turn around and comfort her. Because I wanted nothing more than to make her happy. To make my butterfly spread her wings. But I couldn't prostrate myself before her any more than I already had.

I loved her.

She was the only person I'd ever wanted.

But she needed to make that choice. She needed to be the one to decide if this was what she really wanted. It would kill me if she decided that, in the end, she didn't want this, too. But I couldn't have the tug-of-war. Not anymore. Not after New York.

I snatched my jacket off the hook, glanced once more over my shoulder, and then carefully left the house and the love of my life behind.

Nineteen

David

I wasn't thinking straight as I barreled out of Sutton's house. I didn't have a plan. I had no idea where to go or what to do. On some level, I'd understood when Sutton said that she wanted to work things out with Linda because I had that same feeling right now. Except I wouldn't back down when she couldn't even tell me if this was what she really wanted.

I rushed out through the pouring rain, even more pissed that it hadn't seemed to slow down an inch. In fact, it seemed to be coming down harder. I dashed across the lawn and dropped into the front seat of my Ferrari. Revving the engine, I gunned it out of there.

What I needed was a drink. Or twenty.

I couldn't even fathom how that had happened.

Here I'd been, the fool, rushing over, excited to finally hang out with Sutton and Jason again.

And bam!

Hit by a two-by-four.

There was only one person in town who I could think to talk to about this. And, in that moment, I hated that my boss and closest friend was Sutton's older sister. Because I knew that whatever I said would get back to her in some form or another. Morgan cared too much about both of us not to interfere. And it wasn't like I could call up any of her brothers. They all seemed prime to punch my lights out if I ever hurt Sutton again.

So...par for the course.

With a grunt of frustration, I flicked the windshield wipers higher, shifted gears, and pulled out my cell phone to dial Morgan's number. She answered on the second ring, and I put it onto the Bluetooth.

"Miss me already?" she joked. "Didn't you just leave the office?"

"Yes, Sutton had a meltdown because Maverick's mother threatened to take Jason away from her."

Morgan started laughing, but when I didn't join her, she stopped. "Wait, you're serious."

"Yes."

"That's preposterous."

"That's what I told her."

"Sutton is a great mom, and anyway, no one would ever side with Maverick's parents over the mother of the child. That accusation is laughable."

"She took it personally."

"Well, I suppose she's in an emotionally vulnerable place. The thought of taking her son away probably made her Hulk out."

"She told Linda that she never wanted her to see Jason again."

"That's my girl!" Morgan cheered.

"Yeah," I said, swerving around a car with its flashers on.

"Okay, but so...if that happened, why are you in the car? You are in the car, right? I can hear the rain. It's so fucking loud."

"I am. And I'm leaving because, apparently, that conversation also had Sutton completely second-guess our relationship. She thinks that she should take other people's opinions into account about who she should date and whether she should be happy."

"Oh God, poor Sutton," Morgan said on a sigh. "I don't blame you for leaving, David, but I think she's still pretty messed up about Maverick. And, every time someone gets in her head, it all comes back to the surface."

"I know. Christ, I understand what she's going through. I have been there every step of the way," I said, breezing around someone through the next light. "But, at some level, she has to choose me. We had a great weekend, and then *this* shit again. What more can I do, Mor?"

"I don't know," she said softly. "Wait for her."

"I'd wait for her to the ends of the earth. I'd be happy to even take things slow. But the whiplash is killing me. When we're alone, it's perfect. When we're apart, it all falls to shit. I love her. I want to make this right, but it doesn't seem like there's anything I can do."

"You can be patient."

"I've been the model of patience."

"No one said this was going to be easy. You fell in love with someone who'd had her heart shattered in a way that changed who she was as a person. My sister is not the person she was before Maverick's death. I bet, when you're alone, you make her feel like herself again, and when you're apart, she remembers that she isn't just that person anymore. She is split in two, and only time is going to heal that divide."

I banged my hand on the steering wheel. I knew she was right. I'd known before I walked out of that house. But there was a point where I couldn't take it anymore. And, as much as I wanted to turn this car around and make it right, my pride wouldn't let me.

"Can we go get a beer?"

Morgan slowly breathed out. "Yes. Flips?"

"I'm already on my way."

"Okay, I'll meet you there. And, hey, David?"

"Yeah?"

But I never heard what she was about to say to me.

I was speeding through the next intersection. My mind completely trapped by my problems with Sutton. My phone call with Morgan barely a secondary concern.

Someone laid on their horn.

A flash of bright lights.

I gasped.

Crunch.

A car collided with my Ferrari.

My head whipped to the side.

The airbag deployed.

My world spun.

I heard screaming. "David!"

Then, everything stopped, and I lay still.

Twenty

Sutton

Jason cried in the other room.

I picked my head up from my pillow and ambled down the hallway. He was sitting up on the couch, looking around, confused, as if he wasn't quite sure why he'd taken a nap. I felt grateful that he had.

That conversation with David had been...awful.

I definitely had not wanted Jason awake for that. Or for all the tears I'd had. One horrible conversation had probably been enough for a day, but I'd gone and fucked it up with the second.

Jesus, am I purposely forcing everyone out of my life at this point?

How had everything spiraled so far out of my control?

David and I had been happy. He'd said that. It was true. We had been happy.

Happiness felt like trying to hold on to sand. All you did was watch it slip through your fingers.

"Morning, sleepyhead," I said, hugging Jason tight to me. "Did you have a good nap?"

"Yep," he muttered.

"Good. Ready for some dinner?"

He nodded. I took his hand, and we both walked into the kitchen. I hadn't touched the pizza David had brought over and was now kicking myself. I didn't want to bother in the kitchen, but I knew that cooking something would Zen me out a bit. Let my brain slow down enough to process everything that had just happened.

I went for something simple since I didn't have a lot of energy.

"Breakfast for dinner it is," I told Jason as I cracked a few eggs, pulled out the toast, and started to fry the bacon. I thought about making some brownies later. Baking always did the trick, and I couldn't wait until I went into work tomorrow morning.

The eggs were on the stove when I heard my phone going off in the other room. Jason had pulled all the pots and pans out of the bottom cabinets, and he was banging them together. He'd be occupied with that for probably twenty full seconds at least.

I dashed into the room and grabbed my phone. I saw Morgan was calling. Just great. David must have spoken to her after he left. The last thing I wanted was to deal with her right now, but I wasn't the kind of person to ignore her call.

I sighed dramatically and then answered, "Hey, if you're going to try to talk to me about David, now is not the time."

"Sutton, oh my God, thank God you answered."

The panic in her voice was unmistakable. I'd never heard Morgan sound that scared before.

the WRIGHT ONE

Immediately, my heart started racing, and my throat closed up.

"What's going on? Are you okay?"

"I'm fine. It's David," she gasped. She sounded like she was crying. *Morgan* was crying. "We were on the phone, and he got into a car accident. Someone found the phone and called me back because I was his last contact. He's being taken into the Medical Center."

The phone nearly slipped through my fingers.

Stark terror raced through me.

Panic and desperation and fear. Straight fear.

A black hole had opened up around me and swallowed me whole.

The hospital. He'd been...taken to the hospital.

No. No, no, no. Goddamn it, no!

I wouldn't go back to that place. I wouldn't be there to see another person I loved die. Another person just gone. It wasn't possible.

There was ringing in my ears. The outside world vanished, and just emptiness filled my body. I might throw up, but all I did was stand there in horror.

This couldn't be happening.

This couldn't be happening...again.

How is this my life?

"Sutton! Sutton, are you there?" Morgan called into the phone. "Sutton, please, answer me. I'm on my way to the hospital. Do you need me to come get you?"

That last part snapped me out of the spiral I had been falling down.

"No," I whispered, my voice suddenly hoarse. "I'll meet you there. I have to bring Jason."

"Okay. You're sure you can drive?"

"Yeah," I lied.

I wasn't entirely sure I could drive. Or function as a human being for that matter.

All I remembered was Annie racing toward me on the Fourth of July, calling out to me to let me know that Maverick had collapsed. Then, the mad dash to the hospital. I hadn't even known then what was going on. I had just been nervous. It'd made no sense that he'd collapsed. He had been perfectly healthy. He had been a marathoner, for Christ's sake. He must have been dehydrated or something. But I couldn't figure out why he'd go to the hospital for that.

But, by the time I had gotten to the hospital, it was too late. Heart failure. No one could have seen it coming.

He was gone.

Gone as if he had left for the afternoon and would be back for dinner.

Except he wasn't ever coming back. And I'd had a one-year-old in my arms with not a clue as to what to do with my life.

Just numb and shocked.

Death.

A word I'd heard too much in my short life. A word I'd never come back from. A word that had dismantled my existence and left me hanging in the balance.

Thank God for that toddler in my arms. I wasn't sure how I would have gone on without him.

And, now, I needed to bundle him up and rush him to another hospital and pray that we could get me through this, too.

ᴛʜᴇ WRIGHT ONE

We made it to the hospital fifteen minutes later. Jason was not happy about missing out on his dinner, but I packed him some snacks and hoped for the best. Even as I feared the worst.

The last time I'd walked through these doors, I'd assumed it was nothing. I couldn't have that mindset this time. My life didn't account for happy endings anymore.

My stomach twisted as Jason and I followed the nurse's instructions to David's room. By the time I got there, I thought I was going to hyperventilate. I could barely control my breathing and get it together. But I knew I needed to—at least for Jason's sake.

Before I could even knock on the door, Morgan thrust it open. "Oh my God, I was about to call you."

"Yeah, we just got here," I said.

"Hey, Jason!"

He waved at his aunt Morgan, and a grin broke through her tough exterior. Then, she looked back at me, and it slipped away. I wanted to ask how David was, but the words wouldn't leave my lips. All I could do was stand there and wait…and pray.

"Why don't you go on in? I'll stay here with Jason. We'll go get ice cream downstairs. How does that sound?"

"Yes!" Jason cried in excitement.

"Thanks," I muttered.

"Anytime."

My hands were shaking when I pushed the door open and entered the hospital room. My nerves were frayed. I was barely holding on. I didn't know how I was going to do this. How I was going to talk to him. I felt like I was holding on by a thread, and that thread was unraveling.

David was seated on the bed. Not in it, but on it. His arm was bandaged, and he had a pretty wicked bruise forming on his neck and up his cheek where it looked like an airbag had gotten him.

"Hey," I whispered, taking another step into the room.

"Sutton." He glanced up from where he'd been staring at his phone. "I didn't expect you to show up."

"Of course I'd show up."

"I know how you feel about hospitals."

I tried to still my shaking hands, but it wasn't working. The hospital room. The sanitary smell. The white lights. Everything made me nauseated. I hadn't been in one in over a year. And the last one…the last one had wrecked me.

"Do you?" I murmured.

"Yes," he said calmly.

I nodded. There was nothing else to say to that. David always seemed to know more about me than he let on.

"How are you?"

"I've been better." He tried to turn his neck and winced. "Doctor says I have a mild concussion, a serious case of whiplash, and that I'm going to be sore in my neck, back, and ribs for a while. Some glass from the windshield embedded in my arm. They had to take it out—hence the bandage. Airbag rash on my arms and face, but otherwise, I'm fine."

"Otherwise," I said with a tight laugh. It was really more of a grimace than anything. "What happened exactly?"

He shook his head and seemed to immediately regret it. "I was an idiot. The college kid who hit me was an idiot. It was raining. I was driving too fast. I sped through a yellow light, and oncoming traffic tried to turn in front of me, skidding through one of those stupid Lubbock puddles. Hit my Ferrari with his truck hard enough to shatter my windshield, the side window, and deploy both airbags. My car spun in a circle and hit another car before coming to a stop."

I could see it all like watching a movie. The rain pouring down. The college kid not paying attention. David driving in anger, trying to get as far away from my house as possible.

"But I'm fine," he repeated.

"Fine," I whispered.

Fine.

He'd said he was fine.

He was sitting in a hospital bed because of an argument with me. He was here, in a place I could barely stand in, with a concussion, bruises, and so much pain that he couldn't turn his neck. But he was fine. Sure.

"I'll probably get discharged when the doctor shows up. Do you want to stick around?"

"I…" I steadied myself on the hospital table as my brain spun.

I hadn't thought about what to say in this moment. What to do about where we had left things. I'd thrown all my shit in a bag, grabbed Jason, and disappeared. Now, I was here. Standing here with him, and it all seemed so impossible.

Like all my walls were breaking down.

Because I had stopped for a total of one second before dashing over here. No matter that we had been on rocky terms. No matter that he'd stormed out of my house. All that had flown out the window when I heard he was hurt. I'd rushed to the hospital just as fast as I had for Maverick. The same fears had hit me fresh. It was no different. And yet…utterly, incomprehensibly different.

The worst part of it all was the realization that I *was* all in.

He'd asked me if I was.

And, if anything, this had proven it to me like nothing else could.

I was in love with him.

Unequivocally.

Undeniably.

One hundred ten percent.

And I wanted this so much that my heart hurt. It physically ached from the need. From the desire to make this right.

And, at the same time, with perfect clarity, I knew I *couldn't* do this.

Not because of David.

But because of me.

Seeing him here, no matter whether he was dying or not, just brought all those horrible memories to the surface. All of that pain. It seemed contradictory to both feel like I couldn't lose David and to know that I had to. That I'd already lost Maverick like this. I couldn't handle losing David, too. I remembered what it was like to watch someone I loved with my whole heart die. And it wasn't Linda or Austin guiding my emotions. It wasn't just fear clogging my reactions.

It was that I couldn't face the truth.

I wasn't okay. This *was* too soon. And I wasn't over Maverick's death.

I wasn't over any of it.

"Sutton?" David asked. He waved a hand at me. "What's going on up there?"

"I can't do this," I finally said. "It's not...fair to you."

"Sutton, please..."

"We should break up."

David's jaw went slack. "You're not serious."

"I've been lying to myself. This isn't about anyone else. I've been telling myself it's not too soon. I've been saying that I'm ready. I want to be with you, but you're only getting half of me. And I feel split in two because of it."

"No, no, no," he said. "We can fix this. We can work on this together."

I took a step back. "No, we can't. You can't fix what's already broken."

David was about to open his mouth again, but right then, the doctor walked in. "All right, David Calloway, let me take a look at your file here."

"I'll...talk to you later."

"Sutton, wait."

But I didn't wait. I hurried past the startled doctor and out into the hallway. I knew I'd done the right thing, but somehow...I felt even worse.

Twenty-One

David

The doctor discharged me ten minutes after Sutton left.

But, oddly enough, I didn't feel any better.

I felt like my heart had been run over a cheese grater.

And the worst part was that I understood where she was coming from. I knew exactly where she was in her grieving journey. I'd known from the start that it might be too soon for her, and still, I'd thought it would be okay. So, now, when it was blowing up in my face, it all made perfect sense.

I was causing her more heartache than happiness, which was the opposite of what I always wanted for Sutton.

Morgan was waiting when I got out of the room. Sutton had taken Jason and was gone.

"Will you take me home?" I asked.

"Yeah," she muttered. It was clear that her heart was in her throat, and that was something for Morgan.

"Don't know how I'll make it into work tomorrow."

"You can have the day off."

"I don't think that's a good idea."

"You got into a major car accident…and your girlfriend broke up with you. I think that's an okay idea."

"Let me rephrase; I don't want to stay home."

She sighed. "Okay."

Morgan drove me home in silence. All I wanted was to crawl into bed and pass out, but the doctor had said that I needed to make sure I was careful with my concussion. Morgan followed me inside and promised to watch over me. I wanted to be alone, but there was no talking to Morgan about any of this. Luckily, after she badgered her way into my house, she didn't ask any more questions or talk about Sutton. She just let me stew.

When pain meds finally kicked in, I was more than grateful. The physical pain subsided, but the emotional toll never let my brain up. By the time my mind finally gave in to the exhaustion, sunlight was streaming into the house.

Morgan was still downstairs when I finally came to. "Do you know how hard it was to wake you up in the middle of the night?"

"You woke me up in the middle of the night?"

"Don't remember? Yeah, I followed doctor's orders and made sure you didn't have serious head trauma. But you seem okay."

She yawned. She must have slept like shit if she'd waken me up multiple time at night. "I'm going to head home and change. See you in the office."

I nodded. "See you there."

I felt clearer than I had in a long time. A perfect dark clarity.

I dressed for work, gritting my teeth as I slid into a suit. I still looked like shit from the accident. But my car looked worse. That college student was going to be in a hell of a lot of trouble for running into my car. I feared for the wrath of his parents when their insurance went through the roof. Maybe I'd be nice and save them the trouble.

My rental car had shown up sometime in my delirious state between being passed out and waking up in a haze of pain meds. It was a sad-looking champagne-colored Lexus, but it would do the trick.

I drove into work and went straight up to my office. It was empty, and I wasn't used to coming here from home rather than the gym. My whole routine was messed up. But it wasn't like it mattered.

Sutton was gone.

I had been running from my past as much as she had. Running for a lot longer than Sutton, too. I'd put my family name and my family behind me. Even after I knew that the Calloways were worse people than the Van Pelts. Even after I left for Lubbock. I still hadn't gone back. So, if anything, Sutton had opened that back up for me. And it was time to stop running.

"You look like shit," Morgan said with an arched eyebrow when she entered the office an hour later. She, however, looked perfectly put together.

"I feel like shit," I admitted.

"Well, a truck ran your little sports car over. It seems reasonable that you wouldn't feel too well."

"Agreed."

"I feel like I'm going cross-eyed, trying to catch up on everything so that I can be present for Emery's wedding on Saturday. I cannot believe that it's already here."

"I'm not going."

Morgan sighed. She dropped her bag down and sank into the chair in front of his desk. "Sutton is going to come around to this, you know?"

"I find that highly doubtful."

"She lost her husband. You being in that car accident just triggered every one of her fight-or-flight responses. Freaked her the fuck out, and all she did was react. She is going to be okay."

"She is. Just…not with me."

"I don't believe that. I haven't seen Sutton this happy since Maverick died."

"Happiness doesn't seem to be enough. She has to figure out how to put herself back together without me. I'd like to help her, but I know from personal experience that I can't."

"You already have," Morgan insisted. "You just can't see it right now. She can't see it. But she will."

"That's cheap talk."

"You're not even going to fight for her?"

I launched out of my chair, my back and neck screaming in protest. "Fight for her? That's all I've been doing since day one, Morgan. I have been there every step of the way, as caring and understanding as I could be. I love her. I want what's best for her. But I can't fight for someone who won't let me fight for them."

Morgan lowered her hand, as if to tell me to sit again, but I blew her off.

"I can't do any more than I already have. I'm hurting her more than I'm helping her. And I'm not going to stand by and continue to do that."

"David—"

"I'm resigning."

Now, it was Morgan's turn to jump up from her seat. "No, absolutely not."

"It's a small town. I'm going to see her around. I work for her family. I work for you. It'd be easier if I just left."

"You can't quit. I forbid it."

"You don't have that kind of control."

"I'm telling you that you cannot do this. Go talk to her. Convince her otherwise."

"It would only make it worse."

"Take the week off. Go blow off some steam and think about this. I can't accept your resignation."

"It's too late." I glanced down at my watch. "This morning after you left, I booked a plane ticket to New York for after lunch. I'm going back home."

Morgan ran a hand down her face. "Okay. You know what? Go home. Go back to New York. Think about what it would be like to live in that city again. To live by your family again. I think that'll be enough to bring you back."

"I wouldn't count on it, Morgan." I turned to leave but glanced back at Morgan once. "You're a good friend and a great boss. And I'm sorry it all had to end this way."

"This is not the end."

And she said it with such conviction that I almost believed her.

Twenty-Two

Sutton

"Here you go," I muttered. I passed a cupcake to my customer. "Have a nice day."

The girl gave me a half-smile that was more like a grimace and then hurried away.

"Your people skills are seriously lacking today, sister," Annie said from where she was seated on a raspberry-colored barstool.

I shrugged. It wasn't just my people skills. It was everything.

I felt like I'd been hit by a truck. I had known that severing my ties with David would hurt. I'd anticipated that. But I hadn't expected to feel like I had lost a limb. Like I was slogging through quicksand, trying to claw my way out and only making it worse with every step. I hadn't eaten. I'd barely slept. I was a walking zombie.

"You going to talk to me about it?"

"No." I went about wiping down the counter. It was about to get busy with the lunch rush, and I needed to drink a Red Bull or 5-Hour Energy or something to stay awake. Mostly, I just wanted to go home and cry myself to sleep again.

Because I knew I'd made a horrible, horrible mistake.

I was the master of my own demise.

I needed to find a way to make it right, but at the same time, I knew that I couldn't. That I'd broken what we had. Even if I went to David right now, I didn't know what I'd say. Except that I was miserable without him. And I was so tired of being miserable.

But it didn't erase all the things I'd said.

Or make them any less true.

"All right," Annie said, going back to her schoolwork.

"You're awfully calm."

"Sut, I've been here through it all. I know when to shut up and when to push you. Right now, it's better to shut up and let you figure it out on your own. I think you're already there anyway."

Yeah, my best friend knew me too well.

"I don't know how to fix it."

"You can't. You have to accept how you feel about Maverick and about David. If you don't do that, there's no fixing."

I nodded. She was right, of course. Acceptance was the hardest part. I'd thought I was already there with Mav. But raking my emotions over the coals every week wasn't helping anything.

The bell rang overhead.

"Well, looky here," Annie said.

The WRIGHT ONE

My head popped up, and I saw Morgan saunter into Death by Chocolate.

"Oh God," I grumbled and made a beeline for the back room.

"Sutton Wright, don't you dare," Morgan said. She slapped her hand twice on the counter and tapped her four-inch high heel on the tiled floor.

I stopped in my tracks and sighed. Then, I slowly turned and walked back to the cash register. I plastered on a fake smile for my sister and said, "Welcome to Death by Chocolate. What can I get you?"

"I'll take some of Kimber's famous chocolate cake."

I was glad that she'd actually ordered, so I could busy myself at work and not have to think about what she was going to say to me about David. Because Morgan was here on her lunch break for a reason. I was sure of it.

I passed the cake her way. "I don't want to talk about David."

Morgan grabbed it and a fork and plopped down next to Annie. "Good. I'm not here to talk about David."

I scrunched up my brows and looked at Annie. She shrugged her shoulders, just as confused as I was.

Morgan dug into her cake. I helped three customers as she ate, anxiety eating at me. I knew she wasn't here for cake. And it would come out eventually. I'd had a bad enough week. I wasn't sure I really wanted a lecture from my older sister.

By the time the rush cleared, I was super exhausted. Not sleeping wasn't helping anything.

"Spit it out," I told Morgan. "I know I need to talk to David. I know I was harsh and need to make this shit right. But I'm still totally messed up about what happened."

"You made your position on David perfectly clear," Morgan said. "I'm here about you."

"Me?"

"Seems fair," Annie said.

I pointed my finger at her. "Hey now."

"To be frank, you died with Maverick."

My heart stuttered at those words. At the reality of those words.

"Yes, you've kept on for Jason, but inside, you're dead."

"Morgan," I gasped.

"But you're not dead, Sutton. You're very much alive. You have so many people who love you, and all we've wanted for the last year is to see you happy again. To show that love you've always had shining through you. Maverick would have wanted you to be happy."

"I know. But it's not that easy."

"Of course not. But I've seen you happy with exactly two people since he died. First, with Jason. You want to guess what the second is?"

"I know what the second is."

"Shouldn't that be your answer then?"

"I thought you weren't here to talk about David?"

"I didn't bring him up," she said cleverly. "And, anyway, this is really about you. Because you are standing in the way of your own happiness. Yes, David is my friend, and I don't like to see him hurting, but you're my sister. You've been suffering for so long. I care about you."

the WRIGHT ONE

"She's right," Annie said. "You know she's right."

"Of course she's right. She's Morgan. She's always right."

"I'm not always right, but I am right about this. Why are you doing this to yourself?"

"Because I'm afraid to lose him," I whispered. My heart contracted. "I know I pushed him away, and it's the same thing when it comes down to it. But what if I put my heart on the line, and in the end, he still dies?"

Annie reached out and gripped my hand. "Is he worth taking the risk for?"

Morgan shook her head. "Imagine you were so worried about that with Maverick that you never took that chance with him. You never got married or had Jason. You'd erase all those happy times. Would you do it?"

"No," I gasped. "I'd never want to erase Maverick."

And then it all hit me. What I hadn't seen before in my fear. What I hadn't let myself express, even as I was pushing David further and further away. I would never get rid of those happy moments with Maverick even if I'd known what was coming. I would have held on tighter. I would have demanded more time, more love, more affection. I would have been able to remember the last thing he said to me that day on the Fourth of July. But I couldn't. And it haunted me. The loss of him crushed everything.

But I'd still rather have those few years than none at all.

Why was it different with David? Because I'd already known such heartache? I was trying to protect myself. To keep me from hurting again.

But what I was really doing was erasing that hope for the future. I wasn't clinging tight to the memories that would happen. I wasn't demanding more time. I wasn't stealing more affection. I was foreseeing our inevitable demise and leaning into it rather than clinging to the good.

And *that* was what people meant by Maverick wanting me to be happy.

Not that he wouldn't, of course, want me to love again.

He would have wanted me to cling to life.

That was my happiness. As it always had been.

"If you love him, then you can't let him leave," Morgan said.

I glanced up. "Leave?"

"Didn't you hear a word I said? David tried to quit Wright. He's on his way to the airport to go back to New York."

"Oh my God! He can't go back to New York." Then, I was rushing out from behind the register. "Tell Kimber I had to leave. And that I'm sorry."

"Wait, you're going now?" Annie asked.

"Right now. No time to waste. Thank you. I love you both," I cried over my shoulder as I left the bakery.

I ran full speed to my car around the back of the building. I sped toward the airport, but I knew it was about fifteen minutes to get there. If David had already boarded a flight, I was screwed.

I dialed his number, but I wasn't surprised to find that it went straight to voice mail. Either he was ignoring me or his plane was about to take off. Airplane mode was the devil as far as I was concerned.

The WRIGHT ONE

My panic was going through the roof by the time I pulled into the parking lot outside of Lubbock International Airport. I parked near the front and dashed across the street and through the sliding glass doors. My eyes traveled all around the check-in area. It wasn't a big airport. It would be obvious if he were here. I hadn't asked Morgan how big of a head start he had on me, but it must have been significant if he was already through security.

I found the first airline that had a plane flying to New York City today and cringed as I charged my bank account for an absurd one-way flight. The woman looked at me as if I were insane when I bought the ticket. My lack of baggage probably didn't help anything.

I snatched the paperwork out of her hand and hurried to the security line, which was mercifully short. I impatiently tapped my foot and prayed I wasn't too late.

The person in front of me was probably the most annoying flyer I'd ever met in my life. She didn't know if she needed to take out her iPad, she forgot to take off her shoes, and then her belt went off. And she complained incessantly while it was clear that she was the problem since she couldn't follow instructions.

By the time I was through, I grabbed my purse and hastened to the terminal. My heart skipped a beat when I caught David standing in line for first class to board.

In that moment, he glanced up.

Our eyes met.

And everything felt like it would be all right.

Twenty-Three

David

This had to be a mirage.

It couldn't be real.

Sutton couldn't actually be here.

I'd figured that Morgan would tell her what I was doing, but I'd never imagined that she'd actually show up. And, as much as I wanted to jump with joy, I was guarded. She was suffering. She was grieving. But I had caused it, and I didn't want to get my hopes up that a miracle could somehow happen.

She smiled shyly at me, a blush tinting her cheeks. She looked beautiful. Ridiculously beautiful. She must have come straight from work because she was still in her pink Death by Chocolate apron. She had flour in her hair, which was pulled up into a messy bun. She looked frazzled with dark circles under her eyes, which she hadn't even bothered to try to cover with makeup. She must not have been sleeping. I could relate to that.

I blinked at her twice in confusion, sighed, and then stepped out of line. I walked over to where she was standing. "Sutton, what are you doing here?"

She held up a ticket.

"You bought a plane ticket to New York?" I asked in confusion.

"Yes, well, I had to get through security." She dropped the ticket back into her purse. "You can't go back, David."

"There's not really a reason for me to stay."

"I'm here," she whispered.

"You made it pretty clear that we weren't together."

"I know. I'm not all right. I'm a big mess. I've been through a lot, and it sucks to deal with me right now. But I don't want you to go."

"Sutton…honestly, it's too late."

"Please…"

"You broke up with me. You said that we couldn't be together. That you needed to work on fixing the broken pieces of yourself. I don't think I can help you do that."

"You can't."

I raised my eyebrows in surprise. Well, that wasn't the answer I'd been expecting.

"Only I can fix those pieces, but what I realized is that…I was so busy looking at a possible future of suffering that I couldn't see everything else around me. That my own world wasn't just this grief. I was so into you that I scared myself."

"I have always put you first. And I know you won't believe me right now, but leaving is the right choice. It's good for you."

the WRIGHT ONE

"How could you leaving be good for me?" she demanded.

"Because, as happy as we were, you were twice as miserable. It was like a roller coaster with way more lows than highs."

"That is not true."

"Think about it, and you'll see that it is. I'm leaving for you. I want you to be happy. And all I cause you is heartache."

"No, you're the only thing that makes me happy anymore."

I wished she hadn't said it. Because it was so blatantly false. I'd tried to make her happy. But truth be told, she needed to find happiness with herself again before she could accept it from me or anyone else.

I leaned down and kissed her on the forehead.

"Please," she murmured. "We can make this right."

"This is good-bye."

"No. No, this isn't what's supposed to happen. This is supposed to make it right."

Tears fell down her face, and I gently brushed them from her cheeks.

"I wish I could make this right," I told her.

I really did.

But it was out of my control.

And her running down to the airport wasn't going to change my mind.

"I love you," she whispered.

"Sutton—"

"Don't get on the plane."

"I have to."

"You don't. If you get on that plane, you are going to look back on this moment and know that you were wrong."

"No more tears, Sutton." I shouldered my messenger bag. "This was what you wanted after all."

Anguish crossed her face, but the flicker in her eyes said that it was true. She was the one who had pushed me away. Running up here was too little, too late. I wanted this to magically fix everything, but it wouldn't. We'd just be kidding ourselves if we believed it could.

I hoped I was wrong, but I didn't think I was.

That was why I turned and walked back to the plane.

"David," she gasped.

I closed my eyes against the pain and then handed my boarding pass to the stewardess. She looked between me and Sutton and then put it under the light. It dinged.

"You're all good, sir. Welcome aboard," she said with a touch of sadness.

"Thank you."

I steeled my resolve and walked forward onto the plane. I forced myself not to look back. She could have followed me. She had a plane ticket. But I took my seat in first class, and she never boarded.

As the plane pulled away from the gate, my eyes instinctively looked out the window, back to the terminal. Sutton was still standing there with her face up against the window, still hoping for one last look at me. I knew she couldn't see me, but I could see her. And, as much as I knew I had made the best decision, it felt like torture, wondering.

Was it the right move?

Twenty-Four

David

"Well, that was dramatic," Katherine said when I entered her apartment what felt like a million hours later.

I grunted noncommittally. Sure, flying to New York on such short notice was dramatic, but I didn't care. I was surly and unresponsive. I wanted to punch someone again and also call Sutton right now and apologize. But I wouldn't. Even if I loved her. No, *because* I loved her.

She might have rushed to the airport to try to convince me to stay. Done all the right things to make me not get on that plane. And, still, I'd left because I didn't believe her. I wanted to. But I found it hard to believe that she would really be okay and that we wouldn't turn around a few days later and have the same fight.

She needed to know that I was serious about this. That I would actually leave. All the empty lip service didn't mean a thing when actions didn't back it up.

"And, now, you're growling at me like a caveman. Wonderful," she drawled.

"Thank you for letting me stay in your guest room. I can always go to a hotel though if I cramp your style."

"Stay until you leave."

I almost laughed at her retreating back. My sister...so personable.

"But you have to have tea with Mother," she called from the kitchen.

Ah, no wonder she'd walked away.

"When?"

"Tomorrow. We're meeting her around noon. I told her you had nothing to do since you are now jobless and a vagabond leeching off your relatives."

Even better.

"You're just the best, Ren."

"Aren't I?" she said with her classic false enthusiasm. "Now, I have to go meet Camden for dinner with his parents. So, if I'm not back before midnight, know that I've killed myself."

"Katherine, that's not funny."

"Or he murdered me. One or the other."

"Why are you marrying him? Is it for the Percy name?"

Katherine scoffed. "As if I'd change my last name."

"You could hyphenate."

She pursed her lips. "I'm still proud to be a Van Pelt. Someone in our family has to be."

"But you don't love him."

"And you fell in love, and look where *that* got you."

She slammed the door shut behind her, leaving me alone to my own devices. She wasn't wrong, but she also was...herself. That generally meant she lacked tact. And, right now, she was throwing salt in the wound.

I kicked my shoes off and collapsed back onto her couch.

I felt like an asshole. But I hadn't seen any other option. Walking away was the right thing to do. Even if it had been difficult.

I just needed to weather this. Heartbreak got easier with time.

Or so people said.

The next day, Katherine and I met our mother at an upscale restaurant for afternoon tea. I hadn't been here in a long time. To get in, you had to have a reservation, and to get a reservation, you had to know the right person. All tea was served with finger sandwiches, little pastries, and a glass of champagne for roughly a hundred dollars per person. So that high society could socialize and gossip in private. It was absurd and quintessential Celeste Van Pelt.

"Hello, darling," Celeste said, kissing me on both cheeks before turning to Katherine. "You look lovely."

Katherine frowned. My mother didn't dole out compliments any more than Katherine did.

"Have a seat."

I pulled out Katherine's chair before my own and then sat down, glad that I'd packed a suit before fleeing Lubbock. Otherwise, this would have been much more uncomfortable.

"So, you're back?" Celeste asked. "So soon?"

"Yes, his girlfriend broke up with him. Didn't I tell you, Mother?"

"Thank you, Ren. I can speak for myself."

"Will you ever dispose of that ridiculous nickname?" Katherine asked.

"No," I told her, point-blank.

Katherine arched an eyebrow at me and then hid it as tea was served.

"Well, tell me what happened," Celeste said.

"Do you really care?"

"David, of course I care. I met the young woman, and she was on the unrefined side, but she was sweet. She got you to come back home for the first time in years. I do owe her a debt for that."

Unrefined and sweet. I liked Sutton that way. The last thing I wanted was high-society Sutton. The thought almost made me laugh. Except the laugh was filled with pain and regret. At seeing her pink apron and flour in her hair and knowing it was the end.

"She lost her husband just over a year ago, and she's not quite ready to date again," I honestly answered her. My voice grim. "She thought she was. We tried it out. And it turned out that she wasn't."

"Tragic," my mother said. She carefully added a dash of milk to her tea and stirred. "What a horrible loss."

"Yes. And she has a two-year-old son who she is looking out for."

"A two-year-old?" my mother nearly gasped.

the WRIGHT ONE

Katherine must have not told her everything.

"Yes. He's wonderful actually. But, as you can imagine, her in-laws are not making this easy on her. Her family, while supportive, has high expectations that fall on her shoulders. She carries around a lot of weight, and until she's free of that, I don't know that she'll be ready for a relationship."

"And *you* don't carry around such weight?" she asked carefully.

"It's different."

Katherine laughed softly. "Is it?"

Yes, I had a lot of baggage. Holli's death, my parents' mess, my biological parents' drug addiction, and everyone's expectations for me. But I'd had more time to process that than Sutton had. She hadn't had a year. I'd had eight and even longer than that for Holli.

I was mad that we were here, at this stage. That I'd put myself on the line for her, and she'd shattered it all. But I wasn't mad that I loved her or that she'd helped heal me, too. I was actually more pissed that I hadn't seen it coming. The signs had all been there. Yet I'd let it get to this point.

"Well, are you going to tell me what happened to your face?"

My mother gently touched the bruising on my neck and cheekbone. My back, neck, and ribs still hurt like a bitch, and flying hadn't really helped.

"I totaled my Ferrari."

For the first time, I caught both my mother and Katherine completely off guard.

"You did what?" Katherine gasped.

"It was raining, and some poor college student skidded through the light and totaled my car. It's what sparked this whole mess with Sutton. Her husband had died unexpectedly."

My mother sipped her tea, thoughtful. She didn't dare touch one of the pastries. It wasn't on her diet.

"This is why you should get a driver," Katherine huffed.

"People don't have drivers in Lubbock," I told her.

"Well, they should."

I refrained from rolling my eyes. If Jensen Wright didn't have a driver, then no one in Lubbock needed a driver. In fact, Jensen drove a pickup truck. I bet Katherine would be appalled.

My mother reached out and put her hand on mine. "I'm really glad to have you back, David. I know that our relationship has always been a little rocky. But I admire you for the strong, independent man you are. I love that you've made a name for yourself on your own. Even if I wanted you here. I love your loyalty and passion and drive. You couldn't have gotten where you are without it."

I gawked at my mother. I'd never gotten this many compliments ever, let alone in one sitting.

"But you don't belong here anymore. You should go back to Lubbock."

"What?" I asked in shock. "I'm not going back to Lubbock. Didn't you hear anything I said?"

"Yes. I think you scared this young woman. I think you love her, and you're afraid. And I find that all perfectly reasonable. But Van Pelts do not run from their problems. We face them."

"I do love her. But I left for a reason," I said stubbornly. "I'm not going to just rush back to her. She hasn't even called me or sent me a text message

the WRIGHT ONE

since I left. Not one. The ball is in her court. Not mine."

"The ball is never in the woman's court. Pick up some flowers when you get back into town, and sweep her off her feet."

"Mother, this doesn't even sound like you," Katherine said.

"I don't want you to come back here out of obligation. If you *want* to be in New York, I know plenty of people who can set you up in a firm. We can get you an apartment on Fifth. Life will go on as usual. But you don't want to be here."

"Well, I am here. And I don't want a job in a firm or an apartment on Fifth. I want a fresh start. Because I'm not going back to Lubbock. Sutton and I are over. Whether I want it or not."

I scraped my chair back, already tired of this conversation.

"David, wait," Celeste said. "Don't run out of here in a hurry. I want us to be a family again."

"Then, can we get out of this stuffy room and go eat some real food for lunch? I can't sustain myself on overpriced tea."

"Where do you want to go?" Celeste asked with an arched eyebrow.

I laughed and guided them out of the room. It was a couple of blocks before I found what I had been looking for.

"No way," Katherine said. She looked right and left, as if she couldn't possibly be seen here.

"Dollar pizza." I ordered three slices and handed them off to my mother and sister, who looked as if slapping them across the face would be nicer than handing them cheap pizza.

"If anyone sees me with this, I will probably die," Katherine told me.

"Live a little." I raised my piece of New York–style pizza in the air, as if I were making a toast. "To family and new beginnings."

Then, I took a giant bite of the piping hot meal and watched with both surprise and satisfaction as my upscale mom and snooty sister each bit into their own slices.

Having my family back was a dream I'd never envisioned.

And, while this was amazing, a new kind of wonderful, it wasn't Sutton. I missed her like crazy. And I wondered if a day would ever go by when I didn't mourn losing her.

Twenty-Five

Sutton

I'd stood at that window until the plane was long gone and then some.

He'd left.

I'd laid it all out there, and he'd still left.

I felt...horrible. No, worse than horrible. Like my insides had become my outsides. Like I might throw up at any moment. Like everything in my world had just come crashing down, and there was nothing I could do about it.

Worst of all, I'd done this to myself.

I'd made David think that I wasn't actually ready for this. And he'd believed me. He didn't think I was ready, and running to the airport to stop him hadn't made it any better. In fact, it seemed to have made it worse. Because, now, he was gone for good, believing that all he did was cause me heartache.

Now, my heart was broken.

And I felt as dead inside as I had the day that Maverick died.

David was right. This was about me. Me and only me.

All I knew was that I needed to fix it.

I just had no idea how to do that.

Both luckily and unluckily, Emery and Jensen's wedding was this weekend. So, my Friday night and Saturday were completely booked. I didn't have to think about anything, except the set schedule Heidi had handed out to us earlier that week.

I attended the rehearsal dinner, even managing to laugh at the pictures that were shown of Jensen and Emery together and the stories that Heidi, Landon, and Morgan told about them.

I showed up right on time on Saturday morning. Sat through hair and makeup like a champ. Pulled on the gorgeous red dress Emery had picked out for us. Oohed and aahed over Emery's black wedding dress.

Jensen and Emery met ahead of time. Too anxious to wait to see each other. A million pictures later, everyone was faking their smiles, so I didn't even look out of place.

"Chin up," Morgan said, nudging me.

"I'm happy for them."

"But you're not happy."

I shrugged. "Doesn't matter today. Today is all about Jensen and Emery. This is the wedding he should have had the first go-around."

"True. Colton does look dapper," Morgan said, admiring Jensen's son, who lived with his mother.

"He does. And Jason in that suit," I said with a forced laugh. "So little for such an expense."

the WRIGHT ONE

"It's worth it. You'll cherish these pictures forever."

And they would forever be tainted for me. But, of course, I didn't say that.

It was an evening wedding.

With her black wedding dress and Jensen's tuxedo, it only made sense. They'd chosen a venue just outside of town at one of Lubbock's famous local wineries. Considering how many people Jensen had invited—basically the whole city—they'd wanted something outdoors to accommodate the crowd. And a crowd it was.

The girls and I were peeking through the dressing room space we'd been given and watched as people showed up in droves. The Wright name sure drew a crowd, but everyone knew Jensen. He was well liked and respected. It was showing with how many people were in attendance.

My heart panged at the memory of my own wedding. It had been such a good day. Even as I'd been pregnant and unable to consume any alcohol, Maverick had made it the best time. Now, I was at Jensen's wedding, and the only person I wanted at my side was David. And yet I had pushed him away.

I searched for his face in the crowd even though I knew I wouldn't find it. To my surprise, I saw Penn, who I had completely forgotten was coming to this. But he didn't have Katherine at his side. So, that probably meant no David either.

I turned away from the chaos outside and vacated my spot next to Julia to speak to Emery.

Emery smiled at me and then drank from a glass of champagne.

"How are you holding up?" I asked her.

"Butterflies. I mean, I didn't think Jensen would ever want to get married. Now, it's here, and it's a little scary."

"I know those feelings. But, remember, you're walking toward your future, and that's really all that matters."

Even if your future only lasts for a year and a half.

"You're right," Emery said, downing the rest of her champagne.

I took it from her and placed it on the table.

"I want to marry Jensen. It's just that the theatrics aren't me."

"Enjoy every minute of it. This is the first day of the rest of your life."

Emery grinned wider. "Thanks, Sutton."

"Are you ready? I can help you put your shoes back on."

"Yes. Dear God, why did I decide on such a huge dress? I should be able to slip on my own Converse."

"Because you look beautiful in it, and the Converse kick ass."

I helped her into her shoes as the wedding planner rushed in to get us into position. I grabbed my bouquet of white flowers. Heidi handed Emery her bouquet of bright red flowers. And then we were off.

We meandered through the vineyard before coming to a stop. Our heels sinking into the dirt, we all wished we'd gone with Converse like Emery. Our walk down the aisle was short, but Emery took her time. And it was the happiest I'd ever seen my brother. Their vows were perfect, and somehow, it was all over. It felt like barely a second had passed.

𝓉𝒽𝑒 WRIGHT ONE

The lot of us retreated to the reception space to await the throng of guests. It was an event, and I was glad for the buffet and champagne by the time we made it through the whole thing.

Jason ran over to me with Jenny in tow.

"Hey, buddy. You did so good."

Keeping a two-year-old quiet was magic. I was lucky that Jenny was here. She sank into the seat next to me.

"Mommy?" Then, he pointed across the dance floor to where Bethany was standing with her older sister, Lilyanne.

"Yes, go ahead. You can dance."

I watched him run out onto the dance floor and start to turn around in circles in front of his friends.

"Show-off," I muttered.

Jenny laughed next to me. "He really is. So, how are you holding up?"

"Like shit," I told her honestly. "But I'm here. I'm trying to enjoy the moment for my brother."

"Have you tried calling David?"

"I mean...I've thought about it a dozen times. Picked up the phone, put it down, picked it up again. But what can I say that I didn't say at the airport? It didn't matter then, so how would it matter now?"

"Take the time to process. Maybe he'll come around."

"Maybe."

Just then, Julian appeared and offered Jenny his hand.

"You don't mind?" she asked me.

"Of course not. Go have fun."

Jenny grinned and then rushed onto the dance floor with Julian.

My eyes skittered over the crowd. Jordan had flown his girlfriend in for the occasion, and Annie was giving him the side-eye while simultaneously flirting shamelessly with the bartender. And the rest of my family had smiles plastered on their faces as they danced to the music. Jensen and Emery at the center of the crowd. Landon and a pregnant Heidi laughing together. Austin and Julia not so discreetly mauling each other. Patrick trying to cajole Morgan out onto the dance floor while she rolled her eyes and protested. Even Kimber and her husband, Noah, were out dancing by the kids.

Everyone had someone.

And my someone was thousands of miles away.

I sighed and then stood up. I knew what I needed to do. I couldn't just let David go. Maybe I couldn't fix what I'd broken. But I knew that I missed him desperately. I missed him more than anything. Being at this wedding, alone, only made me realize how lonely I really was. I'd had that happiness, and it had slipped between my fingers. I wanted it back, and the only way to get it back was to make it happen. No one else could fix this but me.

I stood from the table and slowly meandered out of the reception. A few people stopped to say hi to me, but I extracted myself and kept going until I was alone in the vineyard. I pulled my phone out of the pocket of my dress—thank fuck this dress had pockets—and with a big gulp of courage, I called David's number.

It rang three times. Just when I thought for sure that he wouldn't answer, the line clicked over, and he said, "Hello?"

The WRIGHT ONE

"Hey, David," I said softly. I took another step forward, trying to drown out the music from the party.

"This is unexpected."

"I know. I'm sure you didn't think I'd call. And, for a while, I didn't know what the point would be to calling since, you know, you left and went back to New York City, even after I pleaded with you to stay."

"It wasn't the right time."

"Okay, just…let me get this all out there. You don't have to say anything until I'm done." I took a deep breath and launched into my speech. "I have been a widow for four hundred twenty-nine days. And, every one of those days, I have thought jarringly about what I lost. My husband after only a year and a half of marriage. My college friends who couldn't deal with my new status…with my grief. But, most of all, I lost myself. I lost a huge part of who I had been. I couldn't find the joy in anything. I stopped going to church. I was still present at family functions, but I wasn't there. And I kept asking through all of it, *Why me?* What did I do to deserve a dead husband, a dead mother, a dead father? How much more could I take?" I sniffled around the pain, just admitting it all out loud.

"I was drowning, and the only reason I was alive at all was because of Jason. I couldn't let him grow up without any parents either. He didn't even have siblings to raise him.

"And then *you* entered my life. I mean, you were always standing there, on the sidelines, ready to help out whenever I needed you. But I was so far gone that I didn't see it for what it was.

"When I finally opened my eyes, I felt like this was so…right. And the more time we spent together, the more right it felt. I still had doubts and fear, and I was so fucked up. I let it control me instead of learning how to control it. You endured them all and never tried to step away. You were so understanding. So wonderful.

"Then, the car accident happened, and I fell off the deep end. I was drowning again, and I didn't know how to pick myself up. It wasn't until you left…really left that I realized no one else was going to pick me up but myself. I've been so miserable in the days that you have been gone. But I'm not drowning. I just miss you. I miss you so much." I choked up again and hoped the tears wouldn't fall.

"What I've realized is that I put restrictions on myself. I told myself I couldn't or shouldn't feel this way. That little voice told me it was too soon. But it's okay for me to feel again. And it's okay for me to want you. And it's okay to fall in love.

"I'm so sorry for pushing you away. I'm sorry for putting you in a position where you couldn't even believe what I was saying. I'm sorry for everything. I wish that we could fix this. Because I love you. I love you with all my heart. I'll fly to New York tonight if that's what it takes. Because I'm ready for us. I'm ready."

The words hung between us. He didn't say anything at first, and the silence stretched.

"David?"

"Yes, sorry, I could barely hear you over the music."

My heart sank. *He's at some party while on the phone with me? Is this a joke to him?*

the WRIGHT ONE

"What music?"

"Well, it's Michael Bublé right now."

The voice had come from right behind me.

I whirled around, my hand flying to my mouth.

David walked out of the shadows, materializing before me, as if plucked out of thin air.

He extended a hand to me. "Care to dance?"

Twenty-Six

Sutton

"Oh my God, what are you doing here?"

"I realized I was wrong. Something my mom said actually about this being where I belong. Where you are is where I belong. And so I came back to make it right. I was waiting to figure out how to do that without ruining Jensen and Emery's wedding when you walked outside."

I dropped my hand down into David's. My body was abuzz with excitement because he was here. He'd come back. For me.

"I'm so sorry, David. I know I've been so erratic, and I'm not going to promise to never be emotional again. But I do promise that we'll do this together. If you'll have me."

He tugged me forward until our breaths mingled. My red dress nearly touched his tux.

"I'll have you." Then, he bent down and kissed me.

Fireworks exploded.

Church bells rang.

A choir sang.

And, just like that, all the tension and anxiety and worry melted away. I was right where I was supposed to be—in David's arms with his lips on mine. We moved as one, perfectly in sync. My hands pushed up into his hair, and he only tugged me closer, kissing me as if I were a drowning man's air.

I didn't know how long we kissed. It could have been minutes or hours or days. But, when he finally pulled back to rest his forehead against mine and slowly swayed us to the music filtering in from the reception, our breathing was uneven, and my lips were puffy. Thank God for lipstick that didn't budge.

"You're really here to stay?" I whispered.

"Turns out, New York doesn't suit me anymore."

"And Lubbock does?"

"You do."

"I still can't believe you left."

"Me either."

I sighed. "I put you in the position to not believe what I was saying. I was the one with the trust issues, and I made it so that *you* couldn't trust me."

"Shh," he said gently. "No blame. We both did the wrong things. But I just want to be here with you right now."

I leaned my head against his suit and closed my eyes.

We'd gone through the wringer. A roller coaster that had left us both dizzy. But, at the end, when it had come to a stop, there was only me and him. And that was how I wanted it.

the WRIGHT ONE

This wasn't over. We still had a lot to talk about. There would be more ups and downs, but I knew that, if we stayed on the same page, then we could get through it together.

David kissed me one more time before leading me back into the reception. Now that he was here and the dark cloud had lifted from over my head, I felt suddenly like *me* again.

Not the Sutton before Maverick's death.

Or the Sutton after Maverick's death.

But a whole new me.

Sutton with David.

Finally, it felt like my wings had opened, and I was here at last.

We'd only just stepped inside when Linda and Ray appeared before us. I tensed. I didn't want to have this confrontation. Especially not in front of David. I'd been purposely avoiding them through this entire wedding. I didn't want a fight.

"Sutton, can we speak to you?" Ray asked, nudging his wife forward.

"You can go on ahead," I said to David.

But he stood his ground.

"Go on, honey," Ray said to Linda.

She took a deep breath and then glanced between us. "I'm sorry for what I said to you the other day. I was upset. After spending the whole weekend with Jason and then again all day during the week, he just reminded me so much of Maverick. It made it even harder to watch him go."

"I understand that, but that doesn't mean you can threaten me," I told her.

"You're absolutely right. I never should have done that. I swear, I don't know what came over me. Of course, I'm not going to try to take your son from you. You're a great mother, Sutton. I just miss my son so much, and no one seems to miss him like I do."

"I do miss him. Constantly. But dating David doesn't diminish what I had with Maverick, and it doesn't mean that I'm replacing him. It's a new part of my life."

"Ray helped me see that. I get blinded by my grief sometimes."

"I know all about that," I said, glancing at David.

"I don't know if we've been officially introduced." Ray held his hand out. "I'm Ray, and this is my wife, Linda. Figure you're going to be in Sutton's and Jason's lives, so we should be on speaking terms."

"I'm David, and it's a pleasure to meet you. Both of you," David said sincerely.

Linda held her hand out next. "Nice to meet you."

"I know I said that you couldn't be in Jason's life, but I don't want that. I want him to grow up with his grandparents. I want him to have as many people as possible nearby to help him know his dad. But I want us to work as a team. And, if you need to grieve, don't take it out on me…let me be a part of it. Believe me, I have days where it needs to all come out, too."

"That sounds like a deal," Linda said. She had tears in her eyes. "Jason means so much to us. Thank you for forgiving me and letting us see him."

"Thank you for understanding," I said.

The WRIGHT ONE

Then, I pulled Linda in for a hug.

Ray chuckled over our heads. "All right, dear. Let's get out on the dance floor. I know a jitterbug that you might enjoy."

Linda hugged me one more time before taking her husband's hand and following him out onto the dance floor. To my sheer amazement, they certainly did know how to jitterbug.

I laughed. "Wow, they're really good. Who knew?"

David kissed my forehead. "I'm glad that went well. I knew it was weighing on you."

"Thank God you were here when it happened, or I might have blown up on them."

"Then, it all worked out in the end."

"I accept that."

I was trying to steal another kiss when I heard, "Mommy!"

Then, Jason collided with my legs, nearly taking me out entirely. David reached for my arm to steady me, or we both would have toppled over.

"Hey, buddy," I said, ruffling his hair.

"David!" Jason said with a dimpled grin.

"Hey, Jason. How's the party?"

He grinned and pointed at the dance floor.

"I think that's an invitation," I said to David with a raised eyebrow.

"You're okay with this?" he asked.

"More than okay." I took Jason's hand, and David took the other. "If I'm going to have you in every part of my life, just as I am in every part of your life, then it only seems natural that includes Jason. He loves you, and I love you."

"And I love you both, too."

Then, we swung Jason out onto the dance floor.
And, as a family, we danced the night away.

Epilogue

David
Three Years Later

"Stop wringing your hands," I said.

"I can't help it," Sutton murmured.

I reached out and grabbed Sutton's hand in mine. A diamond ring glinted on her left hand. In May, just a few months before Jason had started kindergarten, we'd tied the knot in a small private ceremony on a beach in California. With our collective friends and family around us, it had been magical and beyond my wildest dreams.

"He's going to be excited."

"Am I more worried that he hated kindergarten or loved it? Because maybe, if he hated it, we could keep him out another year. Or better yet, homeschool," she suggested.

"You are not homeschooling him. He loves other kids. It would be a travesty."

"I know," she groaned. "But I miss him even though I work all day, and I know he needs this."

"I was pretty proud that you only cried for ten minutes after he left today."

"Fifteen," she said, a tear coming to her eye. "My little boy is already turning into a man."

I looked skyward. We'd had this discussion already. "He's five, Sut."

"Only thirteen more years at home, and then he'll be going to college."

I put my hand on her expanding belly. "We'll still have this one at home though. And, anyway…that's really far in the future."

"Don't argue with me. I'm pregnant."

I laughed and shook my head at my outrageous wife.

Our honeymoon had been wonderful, and a few weeks later, we'd found out that we were expecting a baby girl in January. Our baby girl. We were still thinking about names. Neither of us could agree on anything.

"Oh, there he is!" She raised her hand to wave, and I pulled it down.

"Don't wave. Wait until he sees us."

"Fine, fine."

We both waited, and to our delight, Jason waved at us and rushed over.

He was turning out to look just like his father. It pained Sutton on occasion to see Maverick shining out of her son, but it also brought her joy. Jason understood as much as he could about what had happened with his dad, but we knew he'd appreciate the information more when he was older.

the WRIGHT ONE

"Mom! Dad!" Jason called. He pulled us both into hugs. "Kindergarten was awesome! Can I go back, Mom? Can I?"

My heart still expanded every time he called me dad.

Sutton choked back her tears and smiled brilliantly. "Of course you can go back! Tell me everything. What did you do? What did you learn?"

Jason recounted his day, giving us a play-by-play of everything he could remember about his first day of kindergarten. Including all of his friends and, of course, that he saw Bethany at recess, who was in another class in the same grade.

I drove us out of the school parking lot and back to our house in the Subaru I'd compromised on. I still had a sports car, but the SUV was way more useful when toting around a kid. Sutton and Jason had moved in with me, and I'd let her redecorate the whole place. It had been really hard for her to sell that place, but it had been her idea since she'd shared that house with Maverick.

"Are we still going to the bakery?" Jason asked.

He handed his backpack to Sutton and followed me inside.

"Yep. We're still going to Mom's work."

Sutton had spent the last three years in culinary school, working on getting a degree as a pastry chef. At first, she'd thought it would be a waste since she worked at Kimber's full-time. But I had known she'd truly love it, and she'd brought new life to the bakery that she was now a co-owner in.

"But, first, we have another surprise for you."

"Did you pick a name for my new sister?"

I laughed. "Not yet."

"I like Addison."

Sutton shook her head. "Remember when you were a quiet kid?"

"No," he mumbled.

"Well, this surprise is in the living room. Let's go."

"Is it a puppy?" he gasped. Then, he sprinted into the living room. "Please let it be a puppy."

I glanced at Sutton with raised eyebrows. "Told you we should have gotten a puppy."

She swatted at me. "This is better."

"The best. What I've always wanted actually."

She kissed me and then walked into the living room.

"There's no puppy."

"Nope. No puppy," I said. Sutton and I took a seat. "It's something else."

"Remember how we told you all of those stories about your dad?" I asked.

"My dad who went to heaven?" he asked slowly.

"That's right," Sutton said. "He was a great man, and we all miss him very much."

Jason looked between us, confused. "But I have a new dad."

"You do. David is your dad, too. And, today…" Sutton said, sniffling as emotions hit her.

"Jason, I want to adopt you," I told him.

"Adopt me?" Jason scrunched his brows up.

"That's right. I want us to be a real family."

"You were adopted, right, Dad?"

"Yep," I said. "I was adopted by your grandma Celeste. And she's pretty great, isn't she?"

Jason nodded his head. "We go on an airplane to see Grandma."

The WRIGHT ONE

"Well, just like Grandma Celeste adopted your dad, your dad wants to adopt you. He wants it so that everyone knows you're his son. Would you like that?"

"Yeah! I want everyone to know he's my dad."

"Well, if you are okay with it, then your dad will sign this paperwork, and everyone will know."

"Yes," Jason said with a big smile, "I want to be adopted."

Sutton started crying and pulled Jason in for a hug. I opened the folder on the table and removed the adoption paperwork. We'd had it drafted weeks ago but wanted to make sure it was the right time. I signed with a flourish.

And, suddenly, it all felt official.

Here I was with my pregnant wife and *our* son.

Jason was finally mine, too.

The End

Want to Read More About Penn Kensington and His Scandalous Life in New York City?

Get ready to lose yourself to the dark and glamorous underbelly of the Upper East Side with a brand-new romance from *USA Today* bestselling author K.A. Linde.

CRUEL MONEY

She was supposed to be a one-night stand.
A way to sate my sexual appetite.
I let her glimpse the man I am. The face that I hide behind my carefully cultivated life.
But she ripped open that divide—
and there's no going back.
Now, she's here. In my city.
I don't care that I'm Manhattan royalty,
and she's the help.
Only that she's living in my summer home. With me.
And I want more.

Acknowledgments

The Wright books have been such a journey. This might not be the official end to them, but for now, we have to say good-bye to this family that has brought us so far. I learned so much from writing these books and can't thank all the fans enough for following along. I pushed boundaries and walked out of my comfort zone for so many of these books while also staying true to the kind of books I love and that you expect from me. I always want to be writing angsty, suited-up heroes with their spunky, driven heroines. And I hope that you come on the next ride with me, too.

So, thank you to every person who has touched not only this book, but also the series. There are so many of you, and I feel blessed to have every one of you in my life.

But, especially to my husband, Joel, who plots all my books with me and has to listen to all the crazy ideas that come out of my head. But you can blame him, too, for some of the hard parts in this one! It's his fault…I swear.

About the Author

K.A. Linde is the *USA Today* bestselling author of the Avoiding Series and more than twenty other novels. She grew up as a military brat and attended the University of Georgia where she obtained a Master's in political science. She works full-time as an author and loves dancing, binge-watching *Supernatural*, and traveling in her spare time.

She currently lives in Lubbock, Texas, with her husband and two super-adorable puppies.

Visit her online at www.kalinde.com and on Facebook, Twitter, and Instagram @authorkalinde.

Join her newsletter at www.kalinde.com/subscribe for exclusive content, free books, and giveaways every month.

Made in the USA
Middletown, DE
05 May 2025